DEAD SERIOUS

"We will be leaving tomorrow to start up a ranch west of town near the Owlhoots. That will be my base of operations. I have a herd of cattle being driven here from Texas. I'm telling you these things, Sheriff, so there will be no guessing on anyone's part. It's not my intention to cause any problems for the townspeople, but at the same time, I will tolerate no interference."

The Sheriff stared at Ashton almost dumfounded.

"You can't be serious."

"I'm dead serious," Ashton stressed.

The Sheriff took his hat off and scratched his head.

"They'll never give you a moment's peace out there. Bullard and his men will bushwhack you or burn you out or both, just as sure as I'm standing here."

GUNBLAZE
Lee Bishop

LEISURE BOOKS   ∞   NEW YORK CITY

A LEISURE BOOK

Published by

Dorchester Publishing Co., Inc.
6 East 39th Street
New York, NY 10016

Printed in the United States of America

1

A black dot appeared on the horizon and parted the sea of golden grass that waved back and forth in the gentle wind. The rider moved forward at a steady pace until he reached the high point in the surrounding sea of grass. The large, powerfully-built man dismounted and rested his horse. John Ashton was not yet thirty, though his face showed the lines of maturity not often found in a young man. Dust covered his clothing, and as he brushed himself off, his brown eyes glanced from horizon to horizon with the careful look of a man always on the alert.

The sun was behind him, rising higher in the east as he came over a small rise and sighted the town ahead of him in the distance.

Ashton smiled, and the hard lines disappeared from his face. His long journey was at an end. For the past several years there had been little time for the simple joys of life. As a major in the Confederate cavalry, he had led his men on mission after mission, blowing up Union railroads in the east, raiding supply depots, scouting for the grey armies, and fighting holding actions so that his armies could retreat.

But it was finished, and he wanted a new life and

new challenges.

The small, southwestern town was a duplicate of many others he had seen. The long main street was crowded on either side with plain wooden buildings that supported false fronts. Ashton rode slowly down the main street, moving only his eyes as he memorized the layout. He noted the location of two bars, a small restaurant, the Sheriff's office, one hotel, and a half-dozen businesses. At the end of the street he turned into the livery stable, dismounted, and stretched. He was glad the journey was at an end and did not care if others knew it. As he had ridden along the street, he noticed people watching him from inside the buildings. They are fearful, he thought.

A tall youth emerged from the darkness of the barn and looked expectantly at Ashton. The thin boy awkwardly shuffled his feet as he shyly grinned at the stranger.

Ashton put the boy at ease by smiling at him.

"Take good care of him. He's carried me a long way," Ashton said in a strong resonant voice.

He flipped a silver dollar to the youth, who caught it with an expert grab.

The youth grinned, showing rows of crooked teeth, and then quickly dropped his head.

"Thanks," the boy mumbled.

With long easy strides, Ashton walked down the boardwalk. He carried himself with an air of confidence and authority. He was sure of himself and of his capabilities.

Ashton opened the restaurant door and walked inside. It was empty except for a Mexican-

6

American waitress behind the counter. He removed his hat and ruffled his thick hair with his left hand. His eyes expressed both friendliness and interest as he smiled. Ashton seated himself and waited until the girl approached the table.

She was about eighteen and wore a simple white blouse and colored skirt. She was a mature woman at an early age. Her breasts jutted out almost defiantly, Ashton thought. Her blouse tapered to a narrow waist, and she had well-proportioned hips and long, brown legs that carried her gracefully across the room.

Ashton ordered breakfast and asked for the coffee first.

"I will bring the coffee right away," she said softly.

Ashton watched her move effortlessly across the room and felt a stirring inside him. I've been on the trail too long, he thought and smiled to himself. The girl reappeared a minute later with the coffee, and they talked for a few moments before she disappeared into the kitchen to prepare his breakfast.

He was sitting at a table near the front window where he could see out on the town. Ashton watched two men as they approached the restaurant. Both were hardcase types, and neither appeared entirely sober. They had both been on an all night drunk, he guessed and now they would have breakfast and a lot of coffee before riding out. The door sprang open and crashed against the wall. The larger of the two men entered first.

An ox of a man, his clothes were disheveled and

dirty, as if he had been in a fight. A massive face, covered with a dirty growth of beard, turned in Ashton's direction. His piglike eyes were bloodshot, and he studied the obvious newcomer with distaste. Ashton calmly returned the stare.

"Maria!" he bellowed and sat down hard in a chair. "Where is that Mexican wench?"

"Go easy, Clay," the second man cautioned.

He joined the giant at the table and sat cautiously with his back to the wall. His eyes darted around the room, settled on Ashton for a moment, and then moved away. He had a long nose and a long, rectangular face that ended with a pointed chin. A prominent Adam's apple moved up and down his long, skinny neck. Ashton could smell the odor of the two men across the room.

"Get out here, Maria!" the one named Clay yelled out.

The girl reluctantly appeared in the back doorway, and the fear in her eyes was evident. The black haired giant's eyes squinted at the girl and moved over her features. His mouth dropped open slightly, and his eyes narrowed as he grinned maliciously at the waitress.

"Come over here," he ordered.

The girl appeared frozen in her tracks.

"Get over here!" the one called Clay yelled again.

With a quick movement of his foot, Ashton kicked over the chair opposite his table. The crash of the chair made both of the men jump. The skinny one with the shifty eyes moved his hand closer to his gun.

8

"You don't have to go over there," Ashton said to the girl.

The oxlike man stared incredulously at Ashton. He was not in the habit of having his actions questioned, and fury boiled in his tiny eyes. His skinny companion began to shift uneasily in his chair, and his eyes continually darted back and forth between Ashton and his partner as he readied himself for action, if necessary. The brute of a man rose from his chair and growled:

"Don't stick your nose in my business."

Then, with surprising speed he moved swiftly across the room and grabbed the girl's arm. Pain registered on her face.

"When I call you I want you now," he roared.

The girl tried to pull away and cried out in pain and fear.

Ashton bolted out of his chair and was across the room in a split second. His right fist smashed into the ox's face, and the giant staggered against the wall, letting go of the girl.

The second hardcase went for his gun, but Ashton had anticipated what the skinny man would do. In one fluid motion, Ashton drew his revolver, whirled, and smashed the shifty-eyed man across the side of the head. He moaned and dropped to the floor.

The waitress screamed, and Ashton turned in time to see the big man awkwardly drawing his gun. Ashton jumped to one side as both revolvers exploded almost simultaneously. Powder clouded the air in the tiny restaurant.

Shot through the heart, the big man let out an

agonizing yell and fell across one of the small tables, crushing it beneath him as he fell to the floor.

The restaurant was momentarily silent, and then the waitress began crying softly as she bent over, covered her face with her hands, and sank to her knees.

This is just what I didn't want to happen, Ashton thought. Damn, why did it have to happen now?

The skinny man came to his senses, rolled over, and stared at his fallen companion. He began to crawl towards him.

"You just shot Clay Bullard. You'll pay for this," he said.

Reaching Bullard, he realized for the first time that the big man was dead. The shifty-eyed one began to shake.

"The old man will hold me responsible for this," he cried out. "Though I didn't have anything to do with it."

Ashton holstered his revolver as the outside door opened slowly, and a cowpuncher poked his head inside.

"Get the Sheriff," Ashton ordered, and the head disappeared.

Five minutes later, the Sheriff, Jim Mayberry, arrived and surveyed the scene. Ashton had already seen to it that the girl was taken care of.

Mayberry, an average-sized man with a broad face and curly, black hair, looked shocked when he saw that the dead man was Clay Bullard.

"What the hell happened here?"

Ashton explained, and during those brief

10

moments Mayberry directed his full attention towards the newcomer. The Sheriff's analytical mind noted that Ashton was quite calm, appeared unruffled by the killing, and spoke in a straightforward manner.

"Mister, do you have any idea who you just shot?" the lawman asked.

"He didn't introduce himself, and I didn't have time to ask," Ashton replied.

"That was Clay Bullard. It's no great loss. But, his father, Jess Bullard, will see you dead as soon as he gets word of what has happened. He lives up in the Owlhoots, the mountains west of here and has twenty men or more up there. They'll be after you in a matter of hours," Mayberry warned.

Slumped over a table at the far side of the room sat Bullard's companion. He struggled to his feet, still groggy from the blow on the head.

"Who is that one?" Ashton asked.

"He's Jake Miles, one of Bullard's men."

Miles' look of unmasked hatred settled on Ashton.

"I want to take him back to the old man. There's burying to be done," Miles said in a hoarse voice.

"Alright," the Sheriff replied. Then looking at Ashton, he said, "Come with me."

The Sheriff was silent and appeared angry as he and Ashton walked to his office. Once inside, he sat down behind his desk and studied the man in front of him.

"You don't need to repeat your speech," Ashton said as he settled into a battered old chair and pulled out his paper and tobacco.

Mayberry's eyes glittered, accenting the wrinkless that crisscrossed his broad face.

"I'm going to spell things out for you," the Sheriff said in a hard, determined voice. "Clay Bullard was no good. He was mean, ugly, and he terrorized a lot of people. He probably needed killing, but has always had his father's protection. Old Jess is just as mean as his son and controls the Owlhoots, the mountains you can see at the end of this grassland. His sanctuary is a bunch of cabins up in the mountains which are protected from all angles. He gives food and shelter to outlaws who pay him to stay there. It's sort of a cooling-off place, if you know what I mean," the lawman said.

The Sheriff stopped talking, took a pipe from his desk, and filled it from an old, leather pouch. Again, he tried to read the young man in front of him, but his analysis was inconclusive. From his many years in law enforcement, Mayberry knew that most men fit into general patterns. Some were cowards, others bullies, and most were hard-working cowpunchers. Ashton didn't fit into any of those categories.

"What I'm trying to tell you is that you had better get on your horse and ride. You'll need all the lead time you can get before Jess starts after you. Any man who shoots his son is a goner."

"Thanks for the warning, but I'm staying," Ashton said in a level voice. "I have business here."

Mayberry came to his feet quickly.

"You're crazy! Didn't you hear what I just told you? You'll be dead before you know it," the

12

lawman exclaimed.

Ashton still appeared unruffled as he slowly exhaled smoke.

"If Bullard is running a hideout for outlaws, why haven't the U. S. Marshalls gone in and cleaned it out?" he asked in a quiet voice.

Mayberry's face flushed, and he angrily stared at Ashton for a moment.

"That place is a fortress. You couldn't get in there with an army. Besides, no one wants to get themselves shot up by trying," said the Sheriff.

"Is everyone afraid of Bullard?"

Ashton's question hit the Sheriff like a hammer. His face turned scarlet, and his chin quivered. However, he was able to pull himself under control and sat down heavily in his chair. He looked out the window at the distant mountains.

"If Bullard comes after you in this town, I'm obliged to see that the townspeople are protected, but that's all. Bullard doesn't bother the people in this town. He's smart that way. He knows that if enough citizens complained, the federal government would have to do something in this territory. What I'm trying to get through your head is that if you want to live, you'd better high-tail it now," Mayberry emphasized.

Ashton smiled for the first time and got up from his chair.

"Sheriff, thanks for the warning and the information. I appreciate your concern. But, the fight was not of my making. However, the next one will be. I'm here in this country to stay," Ashton warned.

2

As Ashton walked along the boardwalk toward the hotel, men passed him but would not meet his eyes. Through the windows of the stores, he could see people staring at him. Word of the killing had spread, and they don't want to get involved, he thought. He entered the hotel.

Behind the front desk, the thin, bald clerk looked both startled and alarmed as Ashton approached. Without saying a word, Ashton signed the register and looked at the clerk, who was sweating profusely.

"I . . . I don't have a room," he stammered.

Ashton stared at him, and his eyes appeared to turn darker.

"Let's not play games. Give me a key to the corner room overlooking the street, now," he ordered in a voice accustomed to giving commands.

The clerk quickly grabbed a key from one of the slots on the wall behind him and placed it on the desk.

"What room does Ben Mathews have?"

"Room nineteen. But, he's not in right now," the clerk responded in a high-pitched voice. "He rode out of town this morning and hasn't come back."

"Tell him to see me as soon as he comes in," Ashton said and walked toward the stairs.

In mid-afternoon Ashton was awakened by a knock on his door. He grabbed his revolver from the small night stand and swung off the bed with a cat-like movement.

"It's me, Major," the muffled voice said from the hallway.

Ashton opened the door and smiled at the tough-looking, barrel-chested man standing before him. Ben Mathews had a white mustache, a ruddy complexion, and light blue eyes that seemed out of place under a thick head of salt-and-pepper colored hair.

The two men greeted each other, and Mathews then asked: "What the hell happened?"

"To set the record straight, the big guy grabbed the girl who was working in the restaurant. I stepped in to help her, and we shot it out. Just bad luck that it happened now."

"The whole town is buzzing with the story. Homesteaders and ranchers are starting to come into town expecting a fight. It kind of reminds me of some of those towns we would go through before a battle," Matthews said. "What do you want to do?"

Ashton grinned.

"The first thing I want you to do is to stop calling me, Major. The war is over. I'm just a man about to start a cattle ranch, so let's keep it on a first-name basis. By the way, are the papers in order?"

The older man threw his hat on the bed and walked to the window.

"Yup. They're in order. You have the land rights to the area that surrounds the water leading from the mountains. Now all you have to do is stay alive long enough to build the ranch."

After a few hours' rest, Ashton's mind was sharp and alert again.

"Relax, Ben. There probably won't be more than three or four men to handle if we have to."

Mathews turned and looked at Ashton. "You got a plan?" he asked skeptically.

Ashton smiled.

"Yes. There is only one main street in this town, and with all the people gathering we should be able to learn how many men are coming in against us before they arrive."

"That figures," Mathews agreed.

Ashton briefly outlined what he planned to do, and then the two men descended to the dining room for an early dinner. The reception there was much the same as it had been on tbe street. All talk stopped as the two men entered and walked to a large corner table. Ashton let bis attention flicker around the room, but no one would meet his eyes.

It's like that, he thought. They must really be frightened of this Bullard. No one wants to be connected with or even acknowledge that he knows Bullard's enemy. It's almost as if they think it will rub off and bring them trouble. The two men ate a leisurely dinner and were engrossed in conversation for nearly an hour.

"How many men do you have coming with the cattle?" Mathews asked.

16

"Randy Miller is in charge of about a dozen men, and a number of them are former Virginia cavalrymen, who fought under a top sergeant by the name of Ben Mathews," Ashton said and grinned.

Mathews' blue eyes sparkled and he grinned.

"Why would they come out here?" the older man asked.

"Most of them had nothing left and were glad to make a fresh start. Brad Prince, Bill Autry, and Jamie McDonald are among them."

"I wish McDonald was here now. He's the best rifle shot I ever saw."

"I made arrangements for them to pick up the breeding stock and the bulls near El Paso and come straight here. They should be arriving in about two weeks," Ashton said.

The two men left the dining room and walked across the street to the general store before closing time. They walked among the stacks of merchandise to the main counter where a young woman was waiting on several customers. Ashton's attention was caught by her long, brown hair that hung almost to her waist. Her hair shone in the light, and her green eyes sparkled as she chatted with the customers. She had high cheek bones, and smooth, well-tanned skin. Ashton watched her as she turned around and pulled supplies from the shelf. She was tall, had a full figure, and carried herself with the easy movements of a graceful young girl.

Her gaze shifted to Ashton, and her eyes held his for a moment. They both smiled. Ashton waited his turn and then approached the counter.

"Hello," she said. "You must be new in town. We haven't met before."

Ashton removed his hat and introduced himself. Immediately, the smile left her face, and he guessed that she associated his name with the killing earlier in the day. He smiled as they talked and the girl began to respond.

"I'm Ann Winter. My father owns this store," she explained.

Her face radiated the simple job of healthy living, and her fresh, direct approach impressed Ashton.

"Will you be staying long?" she asked.

"Yes. I intend to build a ranch in the vicinity." he replied. For the first time he announced his plans.

They talked for several minutes, fully engrossed in one another.

Three men entered the store as Ashton told the girl he wanted two boxes of shotgun shells. He paid for the shells and turned to find his pathway to the door blocked by a young, blond-haired man. The two men flanking him were older, experienced cowhands from the look of their clothing. The blond was thin, his face was long, and a massive scowl accented the sullen expression on his face.

"You the tough one that just hit town?" the blond asked.

Ashton could smell the liquor on his breath and recognized the bravado of a young man trying to make a name for himself.

"Move out of my way," Ashton warned him.

The other two cowhands became uneasy, and Mathews, standing on the other side of the room, instinctively moved closer and attentively watched the proceedings.

"Come on Jeff, let's get what we came for," one of the men said.

But Jeff was not listening. His attention was on Ashton, and his mind was made up.

"Mister, we don't like gun-happy strangers in this town. And, I don't like you or the fact you're talking with Miss Winter," the young man snarled.

Ashton's eyes turned hard.

"I don't know who you are or what you want, but back off and move out of my way."

Sensing trouble was near, Ashton was ready when the blond's hand dropped to his side. He stepped forward quickly, grabbed the man's gunhand near the holster, and with his other hand brought the two boxes of shells smashing against the side of his head. At the same moment, Mathews yelled from the other side of the room.

"You other two men stay out of this!" he ordered. His revolver was pointed at the cowmen, and both men froze in their tracks.

The blond groaned and staggered. Ashton threw the boxes of shells on the counter, took the youth's gun from his holster, and dropped it on the floor. He then whirled the young man around, grabbed him by the back of his pants and collar, and walked him over to the door. Once outside, Ashton pitched the man into the street, where he sprawled in the dirt, momentarily stunned. Ashton turned around and walked back into the store.

"You," he said, looking at the older of the two riders. "Who is that kid, and what's wrong with him?"

With a look of distress and hatred mingling on his face, the cowman stepped forward.

"He's Jeff Starbuck. His father, Ezra Starbuck, owns the big spread east of town. I'm Ford Gentry, ramrod of the Star Ranch."

"Unless he grows up fast, he won't live to see another birthday," Ashton said.

"Maybe. But I'll tell you one thing for sure. His father is going to be mighty unhappy when he finds out what you did to his boy, and he is going to be mighty unhappy with me for letting it happen," Gentry said.

Ashton realized the position the foreman was in. He picked up Starbuck's revolver, flipped open the cylinder, and removed the cartridges. He handed the gun to Gentry.

"Pack him out of here, and don't let him get in my way again," Ashton advised.

The men left the store, and Ashton turned his attention to Ann Winter.

"I'm sorry that happened," he said.

Her face had lost much of its color. She stood with one hand holding the other in front of her. Her green eyes were sad, and her gaze had almost a melancholy look. She saw in him what she desired but feared.

"Things aren't always the way they look," Ashton said and walked out of the store followed by Mathews.

An hour later Ashton and Mathews had con-cluded their stroll through the small town, and Ashton had outlined what he had planned for Bullard and his men.

"How soon do you think they'll come?" Mathew asked.

"They could make it sometime tonight if they rode hard. But I would guess that the burying would take some time. I imagine we can expect them sometime tomorrow."

The men entered the Grand Saloon, and the room became quiet as they approached the bar. The establishment did not measure up to its name. Two games of poker were in progress on one side of the room. Several cowboys sat at other tables, and three men lounged at the bar. Ashton and Mathew could feel the tension in the air as they walked across the room. The bartender, a fat, bald man, whose face glistened with sweat, brought them two glasses and a bottle. Ashton let his eyes roam about the room, and he felt both fear and hostility radiate from the men.

A short, powerfully-built man dressed in gambler's clothes approached Ashton and stopped in front of him. The gambler silently appraised Ashton before speaking.

"My name is Bake Lowry, and I own this saloon. You're not welcome here. This town doesn't like troublemakers nor the idea that one man can walk around thinking he is boss over everything he sees. This town is quiet, and the people don't want trouble. Don't come back in here."

Ashton's eyes narrowed, and he pushed himself

21

away from the bar in order to stand quite close to the gambler. The bar owner backed up a step.

"People have tried to push me ever since I entered town. One man is dead and the other has a bad headache. It should be clear to you that I don't push. And threats don't mean anything to me. I want to put you straight right now. When I come into this bar for a drink, I expect good service and a civil tongue in your head. You get in my way and I'll tear this bar apart board by board," Ashton told the gambler in a cold, merciless voice.

The two men glared at each other, and finally the gambler dropped his gaze and moved away. The cowboys had been watching the confrontation, and their eyes showed respect for Ashton.

"Let's take this bottle up to the room," Ashton told Mathews.

After a few minutes, Ashton and Mathews moved toward the door. The gambler again met Ashton's eyes.

"This bottle is on the house," Ashton said in a challenging voice.

When Lowry made no move to take up the challenge, Ashton grinned and left.

3

The sun's rays began their climb over the horizon; greyness around the town began to lift. The buildings cast long shadows as Ashton looked down the street through the window in his room. People began to stir and men walked out of the buildings, looked around, and then went back inside. There was electricity in the air, and a feeling of anticipation hung over the town. Ashton knew the feeling; he had experienced it often during the Civil War.

In a short while he would go down on the street and make his stand. Death was in the air. No matter what inner feelings he had, the rules of the game left him no choice. The love of a son would make Jess Bullard appear, and pride would make Ashton meet him. Pride built men and destroyed them because there was no swerving from the course that had been established. Some men went through life day after day with resignation and avoided conflict. Others, only a few, lived each day to the fullest and took from life every ounce it had to offer. These were the ones who shaped destiny, built the country, and made life work for them. They also were the ones who fought one another for the summit position.

Horsemen entered the town singularly and in

pairs. Ashton studied them closely. Satisfied that none of them were the men he was to meet, he rolled himself a cigarette and relaxed in the chair.

When a battle was coming it made no difference who was right or wrong. Nothing would change the course of events. They piled up until no one was right, and violence flourished until it played itself out. The methods were hard, but they were the only ones left open to men on the frontier. Ashton would stay and fight, or die.

It was nearly an hour after sunrise when a group of horsemen materialized at the far end of the street and slowly rode toward the hotel. In the lead was a huge man, followed by four other horsemen. Ashton recognized Bullard, although he had never seen him before. He studied the giant, who was about fifty years old and rode with the authority of one whose word was never questioned. The men stopped before the Grand Saloon, and Lowry walked out and exchanged a few words with Bullard. The group of men looked in the direction of the hotel.

Now is the time, Ashton thought. A change suddenly came over him that he never could fully understand. Each time he and his men started out on a mission during the war, the same change came over him. The easiness left him, his senses became keener, he was more aware of each sound, his eyesight became sharp and clear, and his thoughts were orderly and in perspective. Now, he rose from the chair, picked up the shotgun from the bag and checked its loads.

Ashton walked down the stairs into the lobby

and glanced at the clerk, who was visibly frightened. Ashton rested the shotgun beside the front door and walked out on to the boardwalk. He leaned against one of the supporting posts in front, crossed his arms, and looked at the men down the street. They, in turn, returned his stare.

Jess Bullard and his men dismounted. The giant had a broad face covered with a full beard. He wore a cruel expression, and his dark, almost black eyes, were merciless. His body was huge and his powerful torso emitted strength that was seldom questioned. One large hand held a rifle that was dwarfed in his grasp. The dark, baggy clothing he wore made his body appear even larger.

To his right stood a tall, somber hardcase. The man wore long, black hair that touched his shoulders and a matching black mustache that hung down at the corners. He had high cheekbones and a long nose. Dark eyes accented his evil appearance.

The men spread out and began walking toward the hotel. Having accomplished what he set out to do, Ashton straightened up, turned around, and slowly walked back inside the hotel. As soon as he entered, he grabbed the shotgun and raced through the hotel to the rear door. He ran outside and straight back to a gully behind the town. Ashton followed the gully in a crouched position so that he could not be seen as he paralleled the main street. After he had gone about fifty yards, Ashton emerged from the dry creek bed and ran to the rear of the saloon. He quickly went around the corner and quietly approached the main street. Ashton peered around the front corner of the buildings and saw that the five men had shifted position.

Bullard stood at the far side of the street next to the blacksmith's shop. Another man stood between Ashton and Bullard, also near the smith's quarters. A third man stood in the center of the street before the hotel, and the other two outlaws were on Ashton's side of the street, but near the front of the hotel. All of the men had their attention directed the other way when Ashton said:

"You're looking in the wrong direction, Bullard!"

All five of the men jerked themselves around and stared at Ashton.

"Before we get this show started, I want you to know your son drew first. There wouldn't have been a fight if it hadn't been for his actions," Ashton said in a calm, steady voice.

Bullard showed no emotion. "It don't make no never mind," the old man boomed in his deep voice.

As if Bullard's voice were a signal, the men in the street reached for their guns. Ashton tipped up his weapon and the shotgun exploded with an echoing boom. The man between Ashton and Bullard was thrown off his feet as the pellets ripped into his chest.

Almost simultaneously, there was an explosion from the roof of the hotel as Mathews revealed his hiding place behind the false front. One of the two men closest to the hotel was thrown forward by the force of the blast that caught him in the back.

Bullard and the other two gunmen were

momentarily confused. Caught in the cross fire, their attention was divided and their aims were not accurate. Bullard fired quickly at Ashton and then fired a rifle shot at the hotel roof. The other two men also fired at the roof of the hotel and then whirled to shoot at Ashton.

Ashton fired again and the second blast from his double-barreled shotgun took the siding away from the corner of the blacksmith's shop just as Bullard jumped out of sight. The outlaw in the middle of the street ran at top speed and dove for cover near his boss. The shotguns had intimidated the gunhands.

The fifth gunman was steadily firing at the false hotel front above him as Ashton drew his revolver and shot the man through the head. He pitched into the dust and lay still. Mathews reappeared above the hotel front and fired the second blast from his shotgun at Bullard and his remaining gunman as they retreated beyond range.

"I think I got another one. They're headed toward the Mexican shanties," Mathews yelled.

A minute later Mathews came out of the hotel and joined Ashton, who was checking the three downed men to see if they were alive. None were.

Ashton and Mathews worked their way around to the Mexican shacks in time to hear two horses retreating into the distance. A group of Mexicans were excitedly yelling in Spanish as he approached them.

"They take my horses," one man explained in broken English.

Bullard and his companion were small figures in

the distance as they headed back toward the mountains.

"Like shooting fish in a barrel. You could tell those boys weren't in the war," Mathews said. "They came walking up like nothing could penetrate them."

Ashton's foreman shook his head from side to side.

Townspeople, homesteaders, cowboys, and older children converged on the dead men. One man removed bullets from cartridge belts of the dead outlaws as souvenirs. Sheriff Mayberry and the town doctor, Leon Henderson, examined the bodies and covered them. Mayberry had the bodies taken to the undertaker minutes later, and the crowd began to disperse. Within minutes, the bars were doing a booming business.

Mayberry then went to Ashton's room in the hotel and knocked. Mathews let him in.

"Where were you when all the shooting started?" the foreman said with a grin.

Mayberry did not appreciate the joke, and his face took on a solemn expression.

"I told you, you would get no help from me. How long are you staying?" the Sheriff asked Ashton.

"That's my business."

Mayberry looked uneasy and shifted his position.

"Some of the leading townspeople have come to me," Mayberry explained. "They are upset, and with good reason. Ever since you arrived it's been unsafe to walk the streets. They're putting pressure on me to do something.''

"Why don't you start enforcing the laws?" Mathews asked.

Mayberry's face turned red.

"I don't have to stand here and take that," the Sheriff growled.

Ashton rose from his chair and walked across to the window. He then turned and looked at the Sheriff.

"We will be leaving tomorrow to start up a ranch west of town near the Owlhoots. That will be my base of operations. I have a herd of cattle being driven here from Texas. I'm telling you these things, Sheriff, so there will be no guessing on anyone's part. It's not my intention to cause any problems for the townspeople, but at the same time, I will tolerate no interference."

The Sheriff stared at Ashton almost dumfounded.

"You can't be serious."

"I'm dead serious," Ashton stressed.

The Sheriff took his hat off and scratched his head.

"They'll never give you a moment's peace out there. Bullard and his men will bushwack you or burn you out or both, just as sure as I'm standing here," Mayberry said.

4

Jess Bullard and his gunman, Breed Satterlee, rode hard across the grasslands heading for his mountain hideout. Satterlee was wounded with buckshot and continually cursed as they rode. It was mid-afternoon before they started up the trail into the mountains, and they had to stop several times for Satterlee to rest and administer to his wounds, which were not serious.

The men rode into the mountain foothills and up a steep, winding trail into the timber country. The trail wound around stands of aspen and pine trees. They came to a clearing with a small pond, and Satterlee washed his wounds. Bullard was silent and stared into the water while he waited.

They resumed riding and reached a sheer, rock wall that rose upward for five hundred feet. The men followed a narrow, rock trail until they reached the rim. Below them was a panoramic view of the forest and the grasslands to the east. A gnarled, old bristlecone pine stuck out from the rim ledge near the trail. The two men then rode down a narrow gorge that wound around the base of several huge rock formations grouped together.

Bullard signaled to a guard atop one of the rock ledges, and the men rode onward into a large, open meadow surrounded by mountain walls. The meadow contained a number of log buildings, and Bullard dismounted before the largest one. Several men were visible in the area, and he signaled for one man to join him. Satterlee walked over to a bunkhouse and went inside.

Jake Miles entered the large cabin and his nervousness was evident as he shifted from one foot to another.

"You want me, Jess?"

"We got bushwacked in that town. They opened up on us with shotguns, and the other three are dead. I want to know more about that man. Go over to the Starbuck ranch and get Jeff. Tell him I want to see him tomorrow," Bullard said in a deep, rumbling voice.

He was seated in a huge, leather-backed chair with his mammoth arms hanging over the sides.

"That's a long ride, Jess," Miles complained.

Bullard's head jerked up.

"Get going and send in Pete Brandt," Bullard ordered.

Miles left, and Bullard continued to sit and brood. He had lost face for the first time and had known fear for one of the few times in his life. Bullard was a cruel, brutal man, devoid of compassion. He built his life on the premise that the strong take from the weak, and he cared only about power. He was an unfeeling giant, who beat others into submission in order to take whatever he wished. Even his son's death did not bother him greatly, and that was not the reason he rode after Ashton. The newcomer had challenged his authority, and he had set out to destroy him.

Underneath the coarse exterior, Bullard harbored a keen mind, and he realized he had made a mistake that would not be repeated. A frontal attack against Ashton was not the right tactic. In his mind he respected Ashton, and this was a rarity for Bullard. But at the same time he realized that Ashton's presence in the country was a danger to him, and Ashton would have to die.

Brandt, a relative newcomer to the Owlhoots, entered the cabin.

"They don't know you around here, do they?" Bullard asked.

"I want you to ride into Summerville and see what you can find out about a man named John Ashton. I want to know what he is doing in this country, what his plans are, and where he's staying. You probably heard from Satterlee that he's a good shot."

Brandt was a large man with a deeply-wrinkled face from spending years in the sun. He had the perpetual squint of a cowboy who had punched cattle over a long period of time.

"I'll do this job for you, but it'll cost you a free month's board up here. I came up here to stay away from people until it cools down. I killed a sheriff in Texas, and there are a lot of people looking for me. I don't hanker to spend much time among townspeople," Brandt emphasized.

"Get back here as soon as you learn what I want to know," Bullard replied.

Bullard and Brandt walked outside the cabin. The big man stood with his feet slightly spread and

32

surveyed his mountain hideout. It was impenetrable. The cliff faces rose for hundreds of feet all around the large meadown, except for the narrow trail that led out. With only a few men, Bullard could withstand an army. Knowing the mood he was in, the other men at the camp did not approach him.

He viewed the camp with satisfaction. A spring, surrounded by small trees, was just behind the bunkhouse where his paying guests stayed. The cook-shack was to the right of the main log cabin where he lived. Corrals were located at the far end of the clearing. Bullard had first found the camp by chance years ago when he was on the run. Two miners were living there at the time, and Bullard had killed both of them when he decided to make it his headquarters.

Bullard had slowly gathered men of the same ilk around himself and over a period of time allowed other men, for a price, to use the mountain hideout when they were being pursued or had a number of reward posters out on them. His hideout's reputation of being a safe place had been widely circulated, and clients came from all over the southwest, and a few from the north country.

For some unknown reason he felt Ashton's presence in Summerville might well ruin his operation. Bullard's eyes were not pleasant to view even when he was acting normal, and as Ashton crossed his mind again they appeared to glow like hot coals.

Bullard was a basically brutal man with an animalistic nature who would do anything to gain his end. Life was a matter of survival to him. He was merciless and at the same time without conscience. Bullard did not make excuses to himself for what he was. He had been born to a brutal life, took to it rapidly and wanted it no other way. He enjoyed his existence. Bullard was free to take what he wanted, to take what he had to have. Men feared him, and he had unending power in the mountains.

As dusk began to settle over the grasslands, Ann Winter rode along the Verde Creek which had its beginning in the Owlhoots. She was dressed in a riding skirt that was gathered tightly around her waist, a matching jacket over her white blouse and a flat-brimmed riding hat. She had ridden horses from the time she was a small girl and was completely at ease on horseback.

She found that her thoughts were on John Ashton. Her interest and curiosity had been aroused, and she had a vivid picture of him before her eyes. His smiling face was a key to his character, his love of life, and his obviously reckless abandon. But when confronted by Jeff Starbuck, he changed completely. He had learned too early about cruelties of man. He had fought too much and was entirely independent. His mannerisms and actions regarding Starbuck indicated that he was deliberately hard and did not care for people. But because of his smile, she knew this really was not true. Inside, he was a lonely man who had fought for too long. She reasoned that he had come west to build a new life following the war and really did not look for violence.

However, his unyielding pride would always cause him trouble. He could not step aside from trouble, and the sense of honor he displayed would be his downfall.

Pride and honor made him wait calmly in Summerville for Bullard to arrive. She saw the workings of his military mind as he planned the battle and carried it out with a savage fury. There was a savage core in him when he was confronted by a dangerous adversary. The lust to kill in order to survive was in Ashton, and it came boiling out on the streets. No quarter was given and none was asked, and at the end of the fight, the man whom all the townspeople feared and hated was in retreat.

The fast-flowing creek cut through a yellow sea of grass on the plains. The grass was broken by low ridges and the creek banks were green with occasional clusters of trees. As the creek rounded a bend, Ann looked up and saw a man sitting on his horse on the ridge to her right. She studied him as he rode towards her and recognized John Ashton. He let his horse drink at the creek in front of her. They smiled at each other.

"Do you often ride out here alone" he asked.

"This country is civilized now. There has not been any trouble with the Indians for years."

"I wasn't referring to the Indians. This country is not very peaceful."

"I can take care of myself," she answered. "Besides, I have a rifle and know how to use it."

"I'll bet you do," he said.

She took note of his good humor and chivalrous

manner. He was taller than the average man and was more solid. Constant riding had made him lean; the reserve of vitality was apparent.

Ashton dismounted and helped Ann from her horse. As they walked along the creek bank, she tossed her head back, and her brown hair cascaded out behind her. Ann's oval face was perplexed as she looked up at Ashton.

"I know so little about you," she said quietly. "Do you mind if I ask you some questions? I really don't mean to pry, but I am interested."

Ashton took off his hat and swept it in front of himself as he negotiated a mock bow.

"I'm at your disposal."

She laughed and her eyes sparkled at his humor.

"Whatever made you settle in this country?" she asked.

Ashton put his hat back on and looked out over the grasslands. Then he turned and fixed his gaze on her.

"Years ago, before the war, I traveled through this country with my father on the way to California. The country was beginning to be settled, and my father had it in his mind to build a ranch. He's dead now, but he instilled the same desire in me. When the war ended, most of us who fought for the Southern cause had nothing left. Our homes were destroyed, our crops were ruined, and there was no money."

As he talked, Ashton's face became serious. His eyes narrowed, and his voice was hard and flat.

"It's quite simple," he added. "There was nothing left and no reason to stay. My idea now is to build a new life in a new section of the country. By making inquiries I found that the land at the base of the western mountain range still was not settled, and I laid claim to the water rights. My father was farsighted enough to make investments in the North before the war. That was the money I used to buy breeding cattle and take possession of the land.''

He stopped talking, and his face expressed the misery of past memories.

She felt close to him and wanted to reach out and touch him. Neither of them spoke. No words were necessary. Then, abruptly his features changed, and he smiled.

''I like this country already. It's open, and a man feels free. There's plenty of water and grass. You can herd the cattle into the higher foothills during the summer and bring them down on to the grasslands during the winter. The possibilities are endless,'' Ashton said.

The prairie stretched for miles. In the far distance the grass ran up against the blue-grey mountains. Above the mountains the white clouds spread across the horizon, as if a painter had used a brush to paint smoky streaks on a bright blue canvas. After the sun began to set, the endless grasslands took on a deep-gold color. Cactus and brush in the distance turned black as the shadows crept forward. The mountains appeared blacker against a pale blue sky.

She looked at him and appeared concerned.

''There are other places to build a ranch,'' she said.

Ashton knew what she was thinking.

"Not for me. I'm here, and I'm here to stay. The people who live in this country are frightened. It shouldn't be that way. No man should be able to control others through fear. Men should be able to ride this country without fear. It's time that someone took a stand."

He spoke frankly, without hesitation.

"Ann, I want to start a new life. It won't be easy. Life isn't easy. All one can do is try," Ashton said.

The smile left him as he saw the worry appear on her face. They stood, looking deeply into each others eyes. The wind swirled her hair across her cheek. As if mesmerized, Ashton reached out and brushed the hair away from her face. Ann raised her right hand and touched his arm. He could feel the pulse beating in his ears, and he suddenly took her in his arms and kissed her. She responded, and for a moment the two of them were lost in each other.

Ashton stepped back and held her at arm's length.

"I'm sorry, I had no right doing that."

"I wanted you to. Chivalry has its place, but we aren't attending an eastern dance," she replied and laughed.

"Come. I'll race you back to the road," Ann said.

5

Ashton and Mathews had spent two days scouting the lower foothills around the Owlhoots, searching for what Ashton felt would be an ideal ranch site.

"That's it, Ben."

The two men sat on their horses and looked down from the foothills upon a broad expanse of grasslands below them. The valley was about two miles long and a mile wide. The east boundary consisted of rolling hills, while the western limits backed up against the mountain foothills. Running along the western edge of the valley was the Verde Creek, and near the center of the grasslands they had found a spring. Ashton intended to build the main ranch house and other buildings near the spring.

"It looks good, John."

"I think so. We can keep the breeding cattle in this valley for awhile. There's plenty of water, and the openness gives us the protection we want. It will be easy to cut down the timber we need here in the mountains and haul it over to the ranch site."

"When do you want to start?" Mathews asked.

"Right away. There's the Mexican settlement near Summerville, where I think we can hire laborers. I have some basic sketches of how I want

39

the buildings laid out at the hotel. Let's camp here tonight and head back to town in the morning.."

A satisfied look came over Ashton's face. Below him was a serene setting, offering him the calm, steady life for which he searched. For the past five years he had known nothing but horses, guns, and continual movement. They camped in a meadow, cooked dinner, and then sat near the camp fire talking.

"In a way, I miss the excitement," Mathews commented. "It was fun."

They were reclining against their saddles , staring at the fire.

Ashton looked at the older man.

"In the early days it was. Jeb Stuart was cunning; his bold maneuvers outwitted the Federals time after time."

Mathews smiled, and the lines in his face softened.

"Remember Brandy Station?"

Ashton nodded his head in agreement. He would never forget the largest cavalry battle of the war. Nearly ten thousand Federals crossed the upper fords of the Rappahannock, and the battle was fought in the open field and knolls around the area where Stuart was camped. It was a confused action as cavalry changed cavalry. Dust clouds rose until it was impossible to distinguish friend from enemy.

It was a vicious fight and began to swing in favor of the Army of the Potomac until Stuart brought in his reserve squadrons. The troopers would charge and countercharge with sabers flashing, and the air

40

was full of dust, pounding hoofs, the clash of steel, and the inhuman sound of columns of men crashing against one another. The Federals finally withdrew and the Army of Northern Virginia had won another battle.

"Nothing was better than that feeling of victory. It seems we won battle after battle. Almost all of them until the last one," Mathews said.

"The union armys just didn't have the leadership or the knowledge of how to use cavalry properly. The Yankee commanders would split up their units and attach them to infantry detachments to be used for picket and courier duty. It was a terrible waste," Ashton said.

"Stuart was cocky, but he knew what he was doing," Mathews said.

Ashton smiled. Stuart was a dashing figure in his plumed hat, but more important, the Confederate general had a knowledge of cavalry warfare that was unsurpassed. His units would attack Yankee supply lines and outposts, break rail lines, and disrupt communications. He was used by General Robert E. Lee as a flashing, steel fist when the grey and blue met. Stuart was a legend of Southern courage, and the mere weight of his name in the enemy camp was equal to a brigade or two. The enemy always was fearful of his units circling behind them, and the Northern leaders kept many divisions around Washington because of such a possibility.

At the battle of Chancellorsville, Stuart even took command of Stonewall Jackson's infantry, after the legendary general was gravely wounded by his own men. The accident occurred at night, when pickets mistakenly thought Jackson's party was the enemy.

"It was time for it to end, Ben. Towards the end, it was pure slaughter to send our troops into battle with practically no food and little ammunition. At least we could ride away when we ran out of shells. The infantry either had to surrender or throw rocks. General Lee did the right thing. But that's over now, and we can look to the future. Instead of top sergeant, now you are ramrod of a ranch that's yet to be built."

The two men grinned at each other.

"This dream of yours is almost an obsession with you, isn't it?" Mathews asked.

"I guess you could call it that."

"Why do you suppose the people in that town act the way they do?"

"They look frightened to me. It's almost as if they don't want us to upset the balance of things. Those first two days were rough, almost as if we were back in the war again."

Mathews poked the fire with a stick, sending up a shower of sparks and said, "It was like shooting ducks in a barrel. We used that decoy trick over and over during the war and shot up more Yankees than I could count."

"It won't be so easy next time. Bullard wasn't used to anyone standing up against him, but he won't make the same mistake again. We'll have to watch our backs."

"Well, I watched your back through a lot of battles. Nothing has changed much."

The following morning the two men rode into the Mexican settlement just outside Summerville. Most of the buildings were of adobe brick, and the two men dismounted in front of the lone cantina. As they entered the Mexican bar, all conversation stopped. Ashton approached the counter and spoke to the fat Mexican standing behind the bar.

"Do you speak English?"

"Si," he responded, but his eyes were full of mistrust.

"I wish to speak to Jose Gutierrez. Can you tell me where I may find him?"

The man's heavy facial features glistened with sweat.

"Why you want talk to him?" the bartender asked in broken English.

"I understand he is a leader in this community. I want to hire some men to help me build a ranch, and I understand he can help."

The bartender studied Ashton for a moment.

"His casa at end of street on other side."

"Muchos gracias," Ashton replied and walked out.

Mathews and Ashton mounted their horses and continued down the street.

"I wonder how good these laborers are, that is if we can hire any," Mathews commented.

"They are good workers from what I understand. These Mexican peons have a reputation for being able to work long hours in the sun and are better at their work than any cowboy."

They dismounted in front of the house, and a man who Ashton assumed to be Gutierrez ap-

43

peared in the open doorway. He was of medium height, was dressed in the white cotton clothing, and wore sandals. Ashton was immediately impressed with his demeanor. His easy manner reflected pride and wisdom, and his open expression conveyed the feeling of honesty and integrity. Gutierrez's deep tan was accented by silver hair and a matching mustache.

"Senor Gutierrez, my name is John Ashton, and I would like to talk to you about hiring some men from this community to help me build a ranch."

"My home is yours. Please come inside."

Gutierrez bowed slightly and led the way into the adobe building. The room had a dirt floor and was sparsely furnished. One end of the room was closed off by curtains. The three men sat down at a small table.

"It would be my pleasure to offer you gentlemen drinks," Gutierrez said with hardly any traces of an accent.

"It would be appreciated," Ashton answered.

"Maria," Gutierrez said in a soft voice. "Bring us glasses, please."

To Ashton's surprise, the girl from the cafe appeared from behind the curtain with three glasses and a bottle of tequila.

The girl smiled and placed a glass before each of the men. Ashton again was aware of her simple beauty, graceful movements, and aura of sensuality that surrounded her. She quickly disappeared behind the curtain again.

"I apologize for bringing any pain or anxiety to your family," Ashton said.

"Think nothing of that Mr. Ashton. It is I who am in debt to you. Great harm might have come to my daughter if you had not been there. There are few men who would have helped a Mexican girl."

"You can count on John to always help a pretty girl," Mathews said.

"My apologies for not introducing my foreman, Ben Mathews."

Gutierrez and Mathews nodded at each other.

After the men finished a round of drinks, Gutierrez asked, "How may I be of service to you?"

"I am going to build a ranch west of town near the mountains. I need workers and was told that you have great influence among your people and might be able to help me. I would pay them whatever is fair."

Gutierrez studied Ashton for a moment.

"What you ask is dangerous for my people. There are bad men who live in the mountains. I fear they shall try to stop you."

"I have men bringing cattle from Texas. When they arrive, there will be enough of my men to protect the workers while the ranch is being built."

Gutierrez looked down at his hands and thought for a moment. His gaze then returned to Ashton.

"I will help you, but I do have doubts. I only hope you can keep your promise and see that none of my people are harmed."

"I will do my best," Ashton said sincerely.

The men talked for another fifteen minutes and settled on the number of workers to be used and their pay. Ashton and Mathews then departed and rode back into Summerville.

"Ben, you can ride back to the hotel if you want. I think I'll stop in at the store and see about buying some of the equipment and tools we will need."

"Couldn't be another reason you want to stop at the store?" Mathews said.

Ashton glanced at him and smiled.

"That could be a secondary reason."

Ashton dismounted and entered the store. Several townspeople were in the store and glanced at him. Ann Winter was not in sight, and he guessed that the older man behind the counter was her father. He waited until the other customers had left and then approached Thurman Winter.

"Mr. Winter, my name is John Ashton."

Winter had a thin face and wore the expression of a perpetually busy shop owner. His lips tightened and became a mere crease across his face when he realized who Ashton was. A look of resentment crossed his face, and his thin body moved nervously behind the counter.

"I came to buy some tools and equipment I'll need at the ranch I'm building."

"I have no supplies to sell you. Nothing at all, is that clear?" he blurted out rapidly in a high-pitched voice.

The disbelief registered on Ashton's features.

"What?" he said in an unbelieving voice.

"You heard me. I have nothing to sell you. Now I have work to do," Winter said. He started to turn towards the back room.

"Hold it right there," Ashton commanded. "Explain yourself."

46

Ashton's hard voice stopped Winter in his tracks, and a fearful look crossed his face.

"I can't sell you anything."

"Mister," Ashton's voice was like the crack of a whip, "start explaining and now."

"There is nothing more I can say," Winter replied in an angry, frightened voice.

Ann Winter suddenly appeared from the back room, apparently concerned over the loud voices. Ashton calmed himself when he saw her.

"Hello, Ann."

"It's good to see you, John. I see you have met my father," she said, but still appeared puzzled.

"Your father just told me he would not sell me any merchandise. Can you tell me why?"

Thurman Winter's face was contorted with rage.

"I don't want you talking to this man," he shouted at his daughter.

From her expression, Ashton could see that Ann suddenly understood.

"Father, I have not seen you like this before. Please control yourself. John, would you step outside with me?"

He followed her outside the store, still attempting to control his temper.

Ann Winter appeared somewhat embarrassed, but turned and faced Ashton.

"I'm sorry about what happened, John. My father is not a strong man, and he has not always made the best business decisions. Several years ago he had financial problems and might have had to close the store. Ezra Starbuck, the big rancher east of town lent my father enough money to pay off his debts and keep the store going. Starbuck has my father's note for a substantial amount of money."

Ashton could tell it was not easy for her to explain and stood silently while she talked. She had the ability to forgive men's weaknesses, and the strength of character to speak honestly about difficult problems.

"Yesterday, Ford Gentry, Starbuck's foreman, came and talked to Dad. I did not hear exactly what was said, but I do know they were discussing you. Dad would not discuss the meeting afterwards, but I assume from what happened today, that Starbuck applied pressure to my father. He could ruin my father if he wanted to redeem the note."

Ashton stared at her, not knowing what to say. Then a sigh escaped from him and his shoulders dropped.

"I understand," he said in a flat voice.

"I wish there were something I could do," she stated in a soft voice.

"This probably stems from the fact that I roughed up his son in your store that day. What kind of a man is Starbuck?"

Ann looked across the street and thought for a moment.

"Ezra Starbuck is a very proud man. He considers himself to be the leader of this community. He is arrogant at times and has the reputation of ruling his ranch with an iron hand. What you did to his son probably hurt his pride."

Ashton glanced past Ann and saw Mathews approaching them at a fast pace. Mathews was mad.

"John, they closed us out of our rooms in the hotel. The Sheriff was waiting when I arrived, and he informed me that the owner of the hotel no longer wants our business," Mathews blurted out.

Ashton's eyes almost closed as he heard the news. The muscles in his face tightened.

"You will excuse us, Ann?"

"Of course. I'm sorry, John," she replied. She walked into the store.

"Who owns the hotel?"

"Sheriff said it is Ezra Starbuck."

"Ben, Starbuck doesn't want us to do any business in this town. He also holds a note on this store, and we can't buy any merchandise here."

Ashton pounded his fist against his hand and shifted his feet.

"Desert City on the other side of the Owlhoots must be about ninety or one hundred miles from here. But it looks like we will have to get our supplies there. I'll wire my friends in the East and have them set up credit at the bank in Desert City. Take the long road around the Owlhoots and hire wagons. Then bring the supplies and equipment back to the ranch site. I'm going to pay a call at the Starbuck ranch and then head east until I find our herd of cattle. We should be able to meet at the ranch site in about a week or ten days."

"Alright, John."

"Stay away from the Owlhoots, Ben. I don't want another confrontation with Bullard until we get settled at the ranch."

"Right."

The men separated, and Ashton walked over to the Western Union office and sent the necessary message east. He then ate lunch at the cafe. Finished, he walked out of the cafe and rolled himself a cigarette. Ashton nonchalantly smoked and was imperturbable as he thought of the day's events. Thwarted at every turn, he was now more determined than ever to build the ranch.

6

Ashton rode across Starbuck's range. It was strange country to him, and he knew he was not a welcome visitor. He memorized the contour of the land, and the condition of the grass, hills, and streams. From his war days it was his usual custom to familiarize himself with every landmark around him. The plain was broken by low ridges, and from time to time he saw cattle grouped together on portions of the yellow sea of grass. He observed the slash of the Verde Creek as he followed the trail that led to the Starbuck Ranch.

He topped a rise and saw the ranch houses about a mile in the distance. Ashton followed the straight trail, and as he entered the ranch yard he directed his horse to the water trough and let the animal drink.

On the porch of the huge two-story house stood Jeff Starbuck, Ford Gentry, and a third man, who Ashton surmised must be Ezra Starbuck. Ashton guessed Starbuck must be in his late forties. The man had a stocky build, a large oval face, black hair, a mustache, and unfriendly grey eyes.

"You're on the wrong land, Ashton," Starbuck declared in a loud voice. "Turn your horse around and get out of here."

"I think you and I should have a talk," Ashton replied. His relaxed mannerisms showed that he was not concerned with Starbuck's power.

"There's nothing for us to talk about," Starbuck said in an antagonistic voice.

Ashton studied the man, seeing that he was proud, arrogant, and overbearing. He was the supreme lord over his domain, and ruled with unchallenged authority. Starbuck was filled with his own self-importance, unyielding in his decisions, a man who would not tolerate weakness in others. He was a man without compassion or friendliness. Ashton guessed that in a showdown Starbuck would falter; deep inside the man was a coward.

"I want to know why you pulled the strings on Winter so that I couldn't buy supplies."

"What I do is none of your business," Starbuck roared. His temper began to boil over.

Ashton looked at Starbuck, and his eyes bore into the older man. His gaze penetrated deep inside the other man, and Starbuck suddenly felt some of his self-assurance leaving him.

"Starbuck, don't ever get in my way again. I only warn a man once. If you or any of your men cause trouble for me in the future, I will seek you out and make you answer for it," Ashton declared in a cutting voice.

The statement caused both Jeff Starbuck and Ford Gentry to stir. They glanced at the ranch owner.

"If you weren't in my yard, I would shoot you down," Starbuck said loudly.

"A range war or any other kind of war is nasty

business, but if you are looking for a private feud, I'll give it to you," Ashton answered.

"No one talks to my father that way," Jeff Starbuck yelled. He let his hand drop near his revolver.

"Shut up, boy," Starbuck growled.

The young man was embarrassed and his gaze dropped to his feet.

"Ride out of here, Ashton, and don't ever set foot on my land again."

As Starbuck was speaking, a girl of about twenty walked out on the porch. She was strikingly beautiful, and for a moment Ashton's attention was somewhat removed from the three men. She had long, black hair, large dark eyes, and a flawless, cream-colored complexion. Her full lips were parted slightly. Asbton could not remember ever seeing a more beautiful woman. She was dressed in riding clothes that accented her narrow waist, full hips, and long legs.

"Please go back inside, Caroline," her father said.

"I'll stay," she said quietly in a soft, husky voice.

Caroline Starbuck walked to the edge of the porch, fully aware of the impression she made. She was cool, reserved, completely in command of herself and any situation she was confronted with. She studied Ashton and liked what she saw.

"I've heard quite a lot about you since you arrived, Mr. Ashton. It seems you have upset a few people," she said as she smiled.

Ashton could see she was playing a game. She

53

was accustomed to using people for her own entertainment. She was now on stage, and the men around her were the supporting cast.

"It's nice to meet you, Miss Starbuck," Ashton said as he removed his Stetson.

Ezra Starbuck was obviously upset about her entrance, but Ashton could see that his daughter was his prize possession. She was his favorite, so he spoiled her with lavish gifts and gave in to her whims.

"Will you be staying for dinner?" she asked in an innocent voice that was not convincing.

Ashton laughed aloud.

"I hardly think so," he said. Then he tipped his hat, turned the horse, and rode out of the yard.

The four people stood on the porch, all engrossed in different thoughts as he rode away. Starbuck felt unsure of himself and realized that Ashton had strength and ability. A cold hatred for Ashton was mirrored in the son's eyes, while the foreman, Ford Gentry, felt a respect for the newcomer. Caroline, who had overheard everything that had transpired, was curious about him.

"That man is insolent!" Starbuck declared.

Caroline Starbuck suddenly made up her mind and turned to Gentry.

"Saddle my horse, Ford," she instructed.

"You stay close to the ranch with your riding," Starbuck told his daughter.

Ten minutes later Caroline rode north away from the ranch until she was out of sight. Then she turned east along a parallel course to that taken by Ashton and increased her speed until she topped a rise thirty minutes later and saw Ashton to the south of her. She closed the distance rapidly, and when he saw her approaching he stopped his horse.

"I'm unpopular with the Starbucks, haven't you heard?" he said. He smiled at her.

"I've never heard anyone speak to my father that way. He said you were insolent."

"I probably am to some people"

"After you beat up my brother . . . "

"Let's get one thing straight," Ashton emphasized as he cut off her speech, "I didn't beat up your brother. He was drunk. He came into the store and tried to prove what a man he is. After he insulted me, he went for his gun, and he's darn lucky he didn't get hurt."

"That's not the way he tells the story," she said defiantly. Ashton smiled.

"What's so funny?" she said in an arrogant voice.

"For a little girl, you have a big temper."

"I'm not a little girl. I'm a woman," she snapped. "Or haven't you noticed."

"All of the Starbucks seem to have tempers," he said.

She studied him closely, not understanding him. Other men sought her affection and tripped over their own feet in futile attempts to please her. But the other ranchers' sons and men from town bored her. This man was different. He didn't try to please her and even laughed at her.

"There's a dance in town next month at the church. Will you come?" she asked in her most seductive voice.

"I doubt that I will be in town then."

Infuriated, Caroline Starbuck's face showed her indignation.

"You aren't afraid are you?"

Ashton just smiled.

Confused and perplexed, she just stared at him. He was not concerned about her insults, and no ploy seemed to work.

"Why don't we quit playing games?" he said.

She looked at him with judging scrutiny.

"I am agreeable. I hope you and my father are able to work out your differences."

"Right now that doesn't seem possible, but we will be neighbors for a long time. All I want now is to be left alone to get my ranch started."

She glanced toward the horizon, and her perfect profile impressed Ashton.

"You probably will have more trouble with Bullard and his men than with my father."

"I'll handle whatever trouble comes along."

"I think you will."

She wheeled her horse around and glanced back at him.

"Until we meet again, John Ashton?"

"Until we meet again," he acknowledged.

She rode away at a fast pace, and Ashton watched her figure get smaller in the distance.

Two days later Ashton sat on his horse and looked down from a small plateau at the dust cloud in the distance. As the herd approached parallel to his position, he could make out the trail boss in the lead, followed by the point riders. The chuck

56

wagon was out in front of the herd and off to one side. The column was led by a few steers that naturally would go to the front on a cattle drive. The cows and calves fell in behind.

The column narrowed to a dozen head at the front, lengthened, and then stretched into a line that extended for two miles. The twenty-five hundred cattle had been gathered in central Texas and had averaged ten to twelve miles per day on the long march west.

The herd was formed in Texas by rounding up wild, unbranded cattle. Many of the cattle's ancestors had been abandoned by their Mexican owners when the Texans fought free of the Mexican control. In the 1840's there were about three hundred thousand head of cattle in the state.

By the 1860's after the Civil War, their number had grown to more than three million. For the most part, the cattle were unattended and undriven during the war, and it was easy for Ashton to purchase the cows.

A herd of several hundred shorthorn bulls would arrive in another month, and Ashton then would have the beginning of what he hoped would be a cattle ranch that in time would hold thousands of animals.

If all went according to plan, Ashton intended to bring up another herd from Texas the following year. He intended to fatten the animals, once the herd became large, and drive a large number of them north into Colorado each year. The mines and military posts with reservation Indians to feed were a ready market for cattle in the 1860's.

Ashton had left Texas with the herd as it followed the first leg of the Goodnight-Loving trail. After it crossed the Pecos River, Ashton's crew headed due west and left the trail. He stayed with the drive until they crossed the Rio Grande River in central New Mexico Territory and then covered the remaining few hundred miles by himself. Now he was back with the herd and ready to direct it the last fifty miles.

As the long line of the herd stretched out below him, Ashton picked out the point, swing, and flank riders. The men riding drag were obscured by dust and had the most difficult job, that of harassing the lame, weak, and orphaned yearlings to make them keep up. While the trail boss rode ahead to scout for water and pasture, the cowhands rotated among the other positions.

Ashton experienced a feeling of pride as he surveyed the herd. After a few more minutes, he rode down to the herd and waved to the trail boss, Walter Daugherty an experienced Texas cattleman. He had hired Daugherty to bring the cows west and train his former calvary riders in the ways of cattle.

The two men greeted each other, and Daugherty told Ashton the drive had been uneventful except for having to give away a few beefs to the Indians as payment for crossing their land. Daugherty spoke slowly in a deep Texas drawl. He was a big man, nearly fifty, but in excellent condition from his many years on the range. His black hair was streaked with grey, and he had a prominent nose that stuck out between two muttonchop sideburns. His face was bronzed from many years in the sun.

"Them boys is turning into first rate drovers," Daugherty drawled.

"Well, at least you didn't have to teach them anything about horses," Ashton said.

"They ride hell-bent for leather, alright."

"There's only about five or six days left before we reach the ranch site, Walt."

"Did you get everything taken care of?"

"Everything is in order. There was trouble, though, with one of the ranchers in the area, and it looks like there is a band of outlaws operating not far from my ranch."

"Those things are to be expected," Daugherty said in his slow, deep voice. "Texas ranchers are always fighting bout something. And, after you hang a few of those rustlers, that should take care of that problem."

Ashton smiled. He liked Daugherty's practical approach to life, his unhurried manner, and his sensible solutions to problems. The two men rode together the remainder of the day, and one by one his former troopers would ride up and greet Ashton.

The first of the men to greet Ashton was Jamie McDonald, a tall, thin, raw-boned young man with flaming red hair and a large smile. McDonald was one of Ashton's most trusted lieutenants during the war, fearless in the face of gunfire, and a crack rifle shot. Usually, when Ashton had needed a patrol for reconnaissance, McDonald was allowed to pick his own men and head the detail.

McDonald's rate of success was unparalleled.

"Howdy, Major. Been expecting to see you ride up for several days now."

"It's good to see you, Jamie. Have you learned to like cows yet?"

McDonald grinned as he glanced at Daugherty.

"For the first few days those cows got the best of me. They're dumb animals. Never go where you want them to."

Daugherty laughed and said: "He learned fast. All those boys did. Wouldn't mind having them on another drive."

McDonald shook his head in amazement.

"I don't know how you do it, Walt. Year after year in the saddle with beeves."

"The next drive will be easier for you, Jamie. It gets to be routine," Daugherty answered.

"Well, I guess if I can learn to drive cows, I can learn ranch life. How's the ranch situation, Major?"

"I've been having a little trouuble with outlaws, and some of the ranchers aren't too friendly. I'll explain the situation to you boys tonight," Ashton said.

After McDonald returned to the herd, several of the other former cavalrymen rode up and talked with Ashton.

Brad Prince was a serious young man with dark eyes, jet-black hair, and a mustache. He seldom smiled, and Ashton knew the war had left its imprint on him. Both his parents had died during the conflict, and his older brother, an infantry officer, died in combat. Prince was introspective, and his eyes searched for the truth in life. Now that the war was over, Prince had too much time to reflect upon all he had lost. A new life and new experiences would do him good, Ashton thought.

Randy Miller was a short man. He had a broad, deeply-tanned face and smiling eyes. He was the comedian and kept the other men amused with his practical jokes and good-natured kidding.

Bill Autry was tall and thin, taciturn in manner, but extremely reliable. He was second to McDonald in rifle-shooting ability.

The four of them, McDonald, Prince, Miller, and Autry, had become close friends during the war, and although their personalities were quite different, they had one thing in common. They all viewed Ashton with reverence. They regarded him with profound respect and honor and looked to his leadership.

That night Ashton explained to the men what had occurred in Summerville, the battle with Bullard's men, and the problems with Starbuck. The men lounged around the fire as he slowly walked among them. Ashton moved slowly, carried himself with a natural air of authority, yet he met each man's eyes as he passed them, and each felt he was talking directly to him. His intelligence, natural leadership ability, and sincerity had made him a popular commander.

"That's about it so far," Ashton stated as he finished telling of the previous days' events. "The cows will have to be driven over the northernmost section of Starbuck's range in order for them to reach my ranch. There may be trouble when Starbuck learns that we are crossing his land. If there is, no one shoots until I give the signal.''

The men nodded, but were silent. Ashton continued.

''In the coming weeks and months there will be more trouble with Bullard. He will have to be dealt with in time. But right now I want to get the cattle to the ranch, erect the buildings, and form some semblance of order. It won't be easy this first year, and I'm sure you all know that you can leave anytime and that we will still be friends. I didn't anticipate another shooting war, and I'll not order any man to take part in it.''

McDonald spoke up, ''We're in it with you, Major. None of us will leave while you are having troubles. You don't need to bring up the topic again.''

Ashton smiled. He thanked the riders.

Three days later the herd began crossing Starbuck's northern range, and Ashton and his men were continually alert for other riders and possible trouble. Ashton knew the two-mile long herd would not go unnoticed. He was prepared when he sighted the group of horsemen about two miles in the distance. They closed the distance rapidly, and Ashton counted fifteen riders. Starbuck's crew was slightly larger than his own. Ashton's men detached themselves from the long line of cattle and rode to join him.

Ashton's former cavalrymen were arranged in a line beside him and sat on their horses quietly as Starbuck's riders approached. Ashton rode his horse slowly down the line and stopped in the middle.

"See to your rifles," he ordered.

In what appeared to be a long-practiced ritual, the men drew their weapons, checked the loads, and rested the butts of the weapons against their saddles.

Starbuck's riders pounded up to within thirty feet of the line and halted. The dust from the group moved forward, and Ashton could taste its dryness as he breathed. Starbuck's face was livid with rage. The evil in the man's eyes poured out as he looked at Ashton with unmasked hatred.

"I told you never to come on my land again," Starbuck yelled. "Turn those cows around and get them off my ranch or I'll hang everyone of you."

Starbuck was working himself up to a frenzy. Ashton could see that he wanted to fight, and any excuse would do.

Ashton sat straight in the saddle, his hands folded in front of him, his large frame prepared for action.

Ford Gentry was to the right of his boss; Starbuck's son was on his left. The boy was nervous and sweating profusely.

"I order you off my range, now," Starbuck yelled again.

Ashton replied in a deep, strong voice, "I'm taking this herd across your land to my ranch. Any other route would be impractical and would cause us to have to travel around the northern mountain range."

Starbuck appeared flushed with victory.

"Let your guns drop to the ground. I gave you

fair warning, and it went unheeded," Starbuck said in a loud voice.

Gentry turned his head and looked at Starbuck quizzically. He had studied the lineup of men before him and, being a war veteran, he realized that the opposing men were experienced fighters. He suspected from the shape of the formation that they were cavalrymen.

"Boss, I think . . ."

"Shut up," Starbuck ordered.

The ranch owner was caught up in his desire to destroy, and his own self-importance obliterated everything but his goal. No one questioned his authority, and over the years he had been fed with easy victories over weak opposition. He had always crushed everything in his path.

Now Ashton applied the pressure.

"Old man, are you prepared to die?" Ashton asked. The challenge rang out. "How long has it been since you've drawn on a man? You are old and slow and will be the first one to hit the ground when the firing begins. Say good-bye to your land now, because you will be buried on it before evening."

Starbuck looked stunned. The realization of Ashton's words suddenly penetrated; his self-assurance began to leave him.

Ashton guessed that Starbuck's authority had never been seriously challenged. He had sensed this the previous day.

Gentry thought there had been too much talking and felt that his boss was losing the initiative.

"What'll it be, Mr. Starbuck?" Gentry asked.

64

Ashton answered the question, "He's trying to figure out if today is a good day to die."

The remark cut deeply into Starbuck. His gaze dropped, and the feeling of success that had filled him quickly began to disappear. Doubt took its place. Fear began to creep into the man's consciousness, and uncertainty gripped him. Seconds dragged on, and the two opposing forces sensed the change.

Without uttering a word, Starbuck wheeled his horse and rode in the direction of his ranch. He was slumped in the saddle.

Now the Starbuck riders looked to Gentry for leadership. But the foreman was not about to carry the whole operation himself, especially without authorization. He stared at Ashton with a mixed look of admiration and hatred for what he had done to the Starbuck ranch and its name. Gentry realized that a new power had emerged.

The two men stared at each other for several seconds. Ashton admired the courage and intelligence he saw in the other man.

"I'm sorry it had to be this way, Ford," Ashton said.

"What's done is done," Gentry replied.

With that statement, he turned his horse and ordered the men to follow him. Gentry had turned total defeat into more of a standoff for the sake of his riders, whose loyalty was to their ranch and employers.

Ashton and his men remained in their fixed positions until the Starbuck riders were a quarter of a mile away. McDonald moved his horse alongside

Ashton.

"How did you know he was a coward?" McDonald asked.

"Sometimes you can just sense that deep down they don't have what it takes. He's been riding on reputation for too many years," Ashton said.

"When he gets to thinking about what happened and his loss of face, he will be dangerous," McDonald declared.

Ashton nodded in agreement.

7

From the large ranch house porch Caroline Starbuck watched her father ride up. She was concerned over why he was alone, and as she watched him dismount she saw that he was almost in a trance. He appeared to have aged ten years since he rode away from the ranch earlier in the day. The lines in his face were pronounced, he appeared very tired, and his steps were unsure. Starbuck walked by his daughter without even acknowledging her presence and went to his study.

Fifteen minutes later the Starbuck hands, led by Ford Gentry, rode up to the ranch buildings and dismounted.

"What happened, Ford? Father looks terrible." Jeff Starbuck interjected before Gentry could answer.

"Ashton backed him down. That's what happened. Ashton sat on his horse right in front of paw and told him he'd kill him first thing if any shooting broke out. Paw did nothing and then turned his horse and rode away."

"That's enough, Jeff," Gentry warned him.

The young man looked at the foreman with contempt.

"And, why didn't you make a play. The men

were looking to you. What happened to your courage, Gentry?''

The foreman's eyes blazed, but he checked himself.

"I couldn't start a range war without your father's say so. You know that. Now git along,'' Gentry said in a mean voice.

Jeff Starbuck looked at the foreman for a moment and realized he wasn't fooling. He turned and walked into the ranchhouse.

Caroline stared out at the grasslands.

"I'm glad there wasn't any shooting,'' she said.

Gentry was silent for a moment and then turned his attention to her.

"We've lost face. It will be tough to live with for awhile. I only hope your dad doesn't go off the deep-end over this,'' he said with genuine concern.

She smiled at Gentry.

"He will get over it, Ford.''

Gentry said nothing as he slowly rolled himself a cigarette. Caroline studied him and felt secure in the knowledge that Gentry was completely loyal to the Starbuck ranch and its owners. He was the steadying influence, the buffer between the cowboys and her father. If her father made a rash decision, Gentry usually could talk with him and get him to change his mind later. She had grown up on this ranch, and it seemed as if Gentry had always been here. Her mother had divorced her father when she was a young child, and moved to San Francisco. Starbuck's pride had not let him give up the children, and Gentry had become their guardian. He taught them the ways of ranching, and saw to it that their upbringing was proper. She did not put on airs with Gentry, because she knew he understood her and was impervious to her feminine wiles.

"What is your impression of John Ashton," she asked quietly.

"He's an enemy of the Starbuck ranch, so he's an enemy of mine."

"What kind of a man is he?"

Gentry did not answer immediately.

"He's tough and he's smart. He doesn't let anybody push him, and he's deadly when it comes to a fight."

"Is he a bad man, Ford?"

Again Gentry was quiet, and his eyes were focused on the range land before him.

"No," he answered softly. "I wish things had started out differently. He might have been a good neighbor."

Gentry dropped his cigarette, and slowly ground it out with the toe of his boot before he continued.

"Your dad's pride got in his way after Ashton roughed up Jeff. By the way, Jeff deserved what he got. Now there's no turning back. We may have a real fight on our hands unless things cool down."

"But he's practically alone," she said.

"Not any more he isn't. He had nine men with him when he faced us, and there were a few more back with the herd. They were rough hombres who didn't look like cowboys. I'd say they fought with him during the war."

Ezra Starbuck appeared in the doorway behind

Caroline and Gentry.

"Ford, send Jeff in to see me," he ordered.

Starbuck had composed himself and his natural color had returned to his face. He acted more like himself, Gentry thought.

The foreman nodded his head and walked toward the corral. Several minutes later Jeff Starbuck entered the house and went to his father's office.

"You wanted to see me?"

"You've had some contact with Jess Bullard in the past," the ranch owner announced.

His son started to protest, but the elder Starbuck cut him off.

"It's alright. I want you to go talk with him and set up a meeting for tomorrow night at midnight at Twin Buttes. Tell him we can be of help to each other, and I have a plan."

Jeff stared at his father, wondering what he had in mind.

"Is there something you want to say?" Ezra asked in an angry voice.

"No. I guess not," Jeff answered. He turned and left the room.

The following night Starbuck and his son warmed themselves at a small campfire waiting for Bullard to arrive. The rock formation, called Twin Buttes, was located on Starbuck's northern range in an isolated area. The men looked up from the fire and stared into the blackness as they heard muffled hoofbeats. A few minutes later Jess Bullard and two of his riders rode into the circle of firelight and dismounted. Starbuck and Bullard appraised each other silently.

"Been a long time," Bullard said in a deep, penetrating voice. "What's on your mind?"

"Ashton is on my mind. I want him ruined and dead if possible," Starbuck said in a voice edged with hate.

The giant closely watched Starbuck and realized that his wounded pride had turned the rancher into a vengeful adversary.

"Agreed," Bullard replied.

"Step over here. I want a word with you privately," Starbuck said. The two men walked to the outer ring of campfire light.

"Ashton has not yet met the other ranchers," Starbuck explained. "I want to build a feeling of distrust among the other ranch owners against Ashton. Here is an idea I have. I want you and your men to round up about a hundred head of my cattle and drive them to the box canyon area up in the northwest section of Ashton's ranch. Tomorrow night hit J.B. Michaels' spread for thirty or forty head. Then take about the same number from Charlie McGraw's ranch, and finally pick up some stock off Race Jordan's place. You will be able to hide them all in the box canyons. When discovered, it will appear that Ashton is trying to build up his herd by rustling stock from the other ranchers. I want those ranchers solidly behind me when the final confrontation comes."

Bullard remained stoic as Starbuck rambled on with his plan. The rancher's eyes blazed in the firelight, kindled by an overwhelming hatred.

"What's in it for me?" Bullard finally asked.

"You can take two hundred head of my cattle and sell them."

For the first time, Bullard's face showed emotion and surprise, but his eyes remained hooded and suspecting.

"Does this change our agreement?" the bear-like outlaw asked in his deep rumbling voice.

"No. Our agreement was that you would not bother the ranchers around Summerville, but anyone else is fair game. Once Ashton is out of the way, the agreement will be back in force again. Remember, you have a good deal, and with my leadership there have been no complaints registered with the Federal government."

"One other thing," Bullard. "Once Ashton is dead, I want his cattle."

"Don't get greedy. When the time comes, you and I will talk about what kind of a split to make with his stock. Right now I want sentiment built against him."

"Why don't we just bushwack him?"

"You can try, Bullard. But he's smart. You underestimated him once, and he nearly shot you to pieces."

"You didn't do so hot yourself yesterday," Bullard replied.

"That won't happen again," Starbuck declared.

Ben Mathews led the string of wagons loaded with supplies and equipment around the foothills of the Owlhoots and into the grasslands to the ranch site. He had hired six guards in Desert City; in addition, each of the drivers was heavily armed.

Each day of the return trip he had scouted far in advance of the caravan, but had encountered no opposition. Now, ahead of him, he could see the cattle spread out along the Verde Creek. He smiled for the first time in several days as he saw Ashton and Jamie McDonald riding across the range land to meet him.

"It's good to see you, Ben. Any trouble?" Ashton asked.

"Naw, John. Everything went smoothly. The bankers in Desert City went out of their way to help me establish credit with the merchants."

McDonald rode along side Mathews, and the two men shook hands and grinned at each other.

"Where did you dig up this young fella?" Mathews said.

"Me and the boys are out here to save your bacon," McDonald said, laughing.

"That'll be the day," Mathews replied.

The three men rode the short distance to camp, dismounted, and poured themselves coffee.

"I see the Mexican laborers are here," Mathews note.

"Tomorrow they will begin cutting timer and hauling it down here for construction of the ranch house and other buildings. Ben, I want you to take six men and act as lookouts and guards for the laborers. Pick three men to stay with the cattle."

"Jamie, tell Brad Prince and Randy Miller that you three will act as cow chaperones for the first week," Mathews said, chuckling.

"I might get to like cows yet. I been sleeping with them for weeks now," McDonald said with a grin as he walked away to find the other men.

"How've the boys been?" Mathews asked.

"Good," Ashton replied. "They are all eager to learn, and they want to build themselves new lives. Also, I don't think they would object to a little action."

Mathews eyes looked out slyly from the net of wrinkles around the upper part of his face.

"They're gonna see plenty of that before the year is out" the foreman said.

A rider appeared from the north, coming toward the camp at top speed. Bill Autry dismounted in front of the two men. He shook hands with Mathews and then proceeded to tell his news.

"Something funny is going on, Major. Last night I heard a large group of cattle being moved into the box canyons. I stayed out of sight until this morning when the riders were gone and then went down and had a look. The cows carried four different brands. The biggest group, about a hundred, had Starbuck's brand. The other three I wasn't familiar with."

Autry drew the three brands in the dirt.

Ashton and Mathew studied them for a few moments. Mathews suddenly shook his head in understanding.

"From what we heard in town, the other big ranches are south of Starbuck's range. They follow the Verde Creek south. It looks to me that somebody picked up cattle from those ranches and made a big half-circle around to the northwest where they hid them on this ranch," Mathews explained.

Ashton thought for a moment.

"Yes, I see. Then someone conveniently tells the other ranchers that I have been collecting stock on the side. It would be hard to live in this country with all the ranchers against me. Pretty clever. Did you see any of the riders, Bill?"

"No, Major. I thought it was best to stay out of sight, and by morning they were gone."

The three men conversed briefly for a few moments, and then Autry departed for the chuck wagon.

"I'm going to ride over to those other ranches today. You're in charge, Ben. Keep a close watch on those laborers, and see that they aren't hurt."

"Don't you think you should take a couple of boys with you?"

"We need all of them here. Besides, nobody knows where I will be riding."

"Well, watch yourself."

Ashton grinned. "I always do."

By noon Ashton was approaching Race Jordan's ranch southeast of the Starbuck Ranch. The Tumbling Left R brand was prominent on the cows and was one of those on the cattle deposited on Ashton's ranch. He rode up to the ranch house and was greeted by an elderly, dignified man, who was flanked by two cowboys. He noticed that the ranch house and other buildings were more modest than on the Starbuck ranch, but were in good repair.

"Mr. Jordan, my name is John Ashton."

A smile came to the lips of the older man. Race

Jordan had snow white hair and a deeply-tanned face. He gave Ashton the impression of being paternalistic, yet kind.

"Light and sit a spell, young fella," he called out.

Ashton dismounted and shook hands with the slender rancher.

"I've been meaning to get around and meet my new neighbors but haven't had the opportunity yet," Ashton told him as they sat on the porch.

"You've been pretty busy from what I hear."

The two men instinctively liked each other and smiled.

"I've had a little trouble here and there."

The older man put a pipe in his mouth and lighted it.

"This country isn't too friendly right now. Seems to have gotten worse instead of better since I settled here years ago. Too many power-hungry men trying to grab everything for themselves, and I don't mean you."

"It's been rough getting started," Ashton admitted. "I ran into another problem that I thought I should talk to you about."

"If I can be of any help, let me know," Jordan offered.

"Last night one of the men I had posted on my northwest range heard a bunch of cattle being moved into the box canyon area. Next morning he checked the brands and found that about thirty head carried your Tumbling Left R brand. Besides yours, there were about one hundred head of Starbuck's cows and about sixty head carrying the

76

Double Rail and Triangle brands. Maybe you could tell me who the latter brands belong to.''

Jordan frowned and tapped his pipe against the chair.

"The Double Rail belongs to Charlie McGraw, who owns the ranch south of here. The Triangle Brand belongs to J. B. Michaels, who has the last big ranch down the Verde.''

"It was too dark for my man to see who the riders were, but I think it was meant as some kind of embarassment for me. I could see where you could get the wrong idea if someone else brought this news to you.''

Jordan studied the young ranch owner.

"I see your point.''

"I'm a little busy building the ranch right now, but next week I could have my men drive the cattle back to your range.''

Jordan rubbed his hand across his mouth as he thought about the situation.

"Might be better if you wait. It seems to me that you've been set up. Let's wait and see who comes to tell me that the cows are hid away on your land. Chances are that's the party who put them there. Then I'll have some sharp questions for him,'' Jordan proposed.

"That's a good idea,'' Ashton admitted and smiled. "I appreciate the way you took the news. A lot of people have jumped to conclusions lately.''

Jordan puffed on his pipe, then looked at Ashton and said, "To be quite frank with you, Starbuck has been heading for a fall for sometime. He fashions himself to be a king in this country, and most of the time he is overbearing toward his neighbors. He's tried to buy me out, and after I wouldn't sell, he's been unfriendly ever since. I was glad to hear you took him down a notch. And that Bullard is a black-hearted devil. He's the reason I run more men on my ranch than I should. I can see where things are gonna come to a head before long.''

"It's nice to find some friendly neighbors,'' Ashton said.

"You won't find many friends in town. It's Starbuck's town, and he controls a lot of the stores plus the Sheriff. But on the other hand Charlie McGraw and J. B. Michaels both feel the way I do.''

"I'll be riding to those two ranches before the day is out to explain the same things to them.''

"You tell them what I suggested. And don't worry about driving the cattle back here. As soon as we've played this game out, I'll have some of my boys and some from the other two ranches come over and get the cows. You got your hands full.''

Ashton ate lunch with Jordan and then rode on the other two ranches. Charlie McGraw, a tall angular man with a thin face and black beard, also was hospitable and agreed with Jordan's suggestions.

"Take care of yourself, boy. You're playing a lone hand, and the deck is stacked against you,'' McGraw warned.

It was late afternoon before Ashton reached the Michaels' ranch. Joseph Michaels was a taciturn

78

man with blue eyes that studied and appraised Ashton as he talked. He was barrel-chested and wrinkled from the sun.

"I reckon I'll go along with Race and Charlie," Michaels stated.

He invited Ashton to stay the night, but Ashton declined and thanked him.

"I want to make it as far as Summerville tonight. I'm busy at the ranch and in a hurry to get back," he explained.

"Your reception in town will be even worse this time," Michaels pointed out.

Ashton mounted his horse and then looked at Michaels.

"Maybe it's time I asserted myself," he said.

8

Darkness fell, and an almost velvet quiet surrounded Ashton as he rode the trail back to Summerville. It was a star-filled night, and he felt a sense of freedom that was complete and satisfying. The beat of his horse mile after mile was a melody.

There was another reason he wanted to reach Summerville that evening. He had a strong desire to see Ann Winter. He held her beautiful, laughing face in his mind. Remembering how the wind on the range had tossed and swirled her long, brown hair, he smiled. He thought of her honest, straight-forward manner, the deep understanding that her eyes mirrored, and her concern for people.

But the mood passed as he topped a rise and saw the lights of the city before him. The silhouette of himself and the horse stood out, and he was alert now, inspecting each deceptive pattern in the dark.

He rode down the main street, tall and loose in the saddle. The light from the buildings flashed across his face as he passed, and people traveling along the boardwalk stopped to watch and whisper as he moved along to the livery stable.

Sheriff Jim Mayberry watched him pass as he

entered his office. Mayberry's feelings were mixed concerning the tall rancher. In a way, he admired Ashton's courage and ability under pressure. But at the same time, he was creating problems that could only end in a range war. Mayberry did not like Ezra Starbuck, but Starbuck controlled the town and paid him well to carry out orders. His orders now were to see that Ashton was shut out of Summerville. Mayberry was getting older, and no one knew it better than the Sheriff himself. Years before he had been a feared and respected lawman. He had risked his life time after time and still carried lead to prove his luck. But now he was satisfied to run a small town, carry out orders, and lead a comfortable life.

Ashton was tired from the long day's ride, and his temper was short. He entered the hotel lobby and crossed it in long strides. The long-necked hotel clerk had a smug look on his face as Ashton neared the counter.

"You have probably heard you are not welcome in this hotel," the clerk said, but the remainder of his speech was cut short.

Ashton's arm shot forward, grabbed him by the front of his shirt just below the neck, and pulled him halfway over the counter. Ashton shook him for a moment, and the man's eyes bulged out and his face turned a pasty white color.

"I'm through playing games. From now on when I enter this hotel I want to see the key to that corner room laying on the desk. Do we understand each other, friend?"

Ashton pushed him back, and the clerk slithered

across the counter on to the floor and stumbled over to get the key. His eyes were open wide and the frightened expression remained on his face as he placed the key before Ashton.

He went to the room, washed up, and tried to rest, but his mind was too active. The work had to be done on the ranch, the placement of the cattle and the ever-present problems of Bullard and Starbuck were on his mind. Minutes later he was going down the hotel stairs and out into the night. Piano music from Lowry's saloon drifted on the night air as he walked toward the lighted windows.

Ashton glanced from one side to the other as he entered the bar. Talk died down as he crossed the room and rested his big arms on the bar top. The bartender brought him a bottle and glass, and he leisurely poured himself a drink. From outward appearances he was calm, but inside his every sense was alert, and he caught the signal that passed between the bartender and Lowry. In a nonchalant manner, the bartender drifted to the end of the bar, placing Ashton between himself and Lowry. As if by mental telepathy, the cowboys at the bar moved away from Ashton. Looking into the long mirror behind the bar, Ashton watched the bouncer standing near the door straighten up and hook his thumb in his gunbelt. By now, the talk in the room had stopped and the onlookers' faces showed anticipation. Ashton knew his position was not good, but he didn't care. He was tired of the games, of the insults, and of the attempts to thwart his entry into the community. He was through being a gentleman, and above all he was mad.

"This town is closed to you," Lowry said in a loud voice.

The gambler got up from the table where he had been playing poker and slowly walked to the end of the bar. Tension filled the room, and Ashton noted that if he turned to look at Lowry, the fat bartender would be directly behind him. Ashton maintained his position so that he could move in either direction and at the same time use the mirror to keep the gunman behind him in view.

"I just opened the hotel," Ashton announced.

"Last time you were in here I warned you not to come back."

"I'm back," Ashton said, and he slowly turned his head and stared at Lowry.

"When I don't want someone in my place, they don't come back."

"I'm back," Ashton said. His gaze returned to the mirror.

"I don't bluff like some people we know."

Ashton grinned. He knew the gambler was not quite sure he had the fire power, even with three men, to accomplish the job.

A man stepped through the bar door, and in the mirror Ashton recognized Jamie McDonald. He had been watching the play build from outside and now moved swiftly across the room and stood beside the bartender. The fat bartender looked at him in surprise, and McDonald whispered to him:

"If you touch that scatter gun from under the counter, I'll blow your fat head off."

McDonald gave the bartender a big smile and

then fixed his attention on the gunman at the doorway. A voice from outside told the bouncer very quietly:

"Stay out of this play."

The gunman straightened up and let his hands drop to his sides.

Ashton now turned slowly and walked toward Lowry. His eyes were hard and merciless as he stood in front of the gambler. Lowry's face showed fear, and he quickly reached inside his coat for the hidden gun. Ashton grabbed his arm, twisted the wrist, and the derringer dropped to the floor.

His right fist smashed into Lowry's face and the gambler flew backwards and landed on a poker table. The table tipped over and fell to the floor amid a shower of poker chips and cards. He shook his head, got to his feet, and rushed Ashton, swinging wildly. One blow landed on Ashton's cheek and he felt the gambler's ring tear the flesh.

Animal ferocity filled Ashton as he savagely struck Lowry in the stomach. The gambler doubled over and gasped for breath. With his left hand, Ashton grabbed his hair and lifted his head. He then drove a straight right hand into Lowry's face that landed bluntly. The gambler hit the floor hard and did not move. The saloon was quiet except for Ashton's heavy breathing.

"You," Ashton said to the gunman near the front door. "Get him out of here." The gunman grabbed Lowry under the arms and dragged him out of the saloon.

"Bartender, the drinks are on the house for

everyone. Start that music," Ashton ordered.

Cowboys flocked to the bar, and conversation rose to a high pitch as the events were recounted by the men. The fat bartender was sweating heavily and pouring one drink after another. Jamie McDonald walked around behind the bar, grabbed two bottles of whiskey and three glasses, and walked over to an empty table. Brad Prince entered the bar from the street and joined the two men at the table. Ashton downed a quick drink and poured himself a second. He felt the tension suddenly leave and the whiskey felt warm going down. Ashton relaxed in the chair and grinned at the two men.

"The boys needed a few supplies, and that was a good excuse to see what the town was like. Appears we happened along just at the right time," McDonald said.

"They had me boxed, alright. I sure was happy to see you walk in," Ashton admitted.

The three men drank freely, joking and laughing for nearly half an hour before Sheriff Jim Mayberry entered. He walked over to the table and faced Ashton. The men in the bar quieted down.

"Doc Henderson said Lowry is pretty banged up. He still doesn't know where he's at or what time it is. You are causing trouble again, Ashton," Mayberry warned.

Ashton grinned at him.

"Drinks are on the house. Why don't you sit down and relax, Sheriff."

"No," he said solemnly. "I'm closing the bar,

because no one is here to run it. And it'll stay closed until Lowry is back on his feet again."

Murmurs of disapproval came from the cowboys along the bar.

"Well, I guess we'll have to take the party over to the hotel."

"The hotel is closed to you and your men," Mayberry announced. "You know that."

"I opened it earlier this evening."

Ashton and his men rose from their chairs.

"I have orders to keep you out of there," Mayberry said.

Ashton moved to him and spoke quietly so that none of the other cowboys in the room could hear.

"If you want to push it, go ahead. But, you'll end up the same way as Lowry, and then every two-bit punk will be trying to challenge you. You will have lost your authority, which will make you useless as a lawman. Starbuck isn't worth it."

For several seconds Mayberrry thought over what Ashton had said. The two men silently studied each other.

"Close the bar, Jack," Mayberry said loudly as he made his decision.

The bartender began snuffing out the lights and the cowboys slowly drifted toward the door.

"Take the bottles over to the hotel," Ashton told McDonald.

His men departed, and Ashton and Mayberry moved out on the front boardwalk together. They stood together and looked out over the town, which was quiet except for a few cowboys who mounted their horses and rode away. Mayberry rolled a cigarette and lighted a match. In the flame's light his eyes were hard as they gazed at Ashton.

"Friend, I'm not afraid of you. That's something you ought to know. I've fought bigger and tougher men and won."

"I know that, Mayberry."

"I don't know if you'll last. Someone may just bushwack you one dark night. But I'll say one thing for you, you have guts."

"Had things been different, Sheriff, you and I might even have been friends," Ashton said.

In the darkness, a slight smile came to Mayberry's face.

On the following morning Ashton swung his feet off the bed and sat up. He flexed his bruised and scraped knuckles, gently felt his cut face, and was immediately made aware of the pounding in his head from the previous night's liquor. He shaved and washed and heard movement in the room next door, indicating that McDonald and Prince were up. He knocked on their door.

"You men ready for breakfast?"

"We thought you were going to sleep until noon," McDonald said, grinning.

After the late breakfast, Ashton excused himself and walked over to the general store to see Ann Winter. She was behind the counter talking to the lone customer in the store when he entered. She glanced at him, but her nod of recognition was noticibly reserved. The elderly woman customer finally made her purchase, and as she walked past

Ashton, her nose wrinkled as if she smelled something distasteful.

Ann Winter was dressed in a bright gingham dress and her hair was drawn back from her face with a red ribbon. Her green eyes held his as he approached her. He thought he detected a restraint and almost a sadness within her.

"I've missed seeing you," he said quietly.

She did not reply, nor did she look away. Instead, her eyes continued to analyze him, as if she were trying to determine if her first thoughts about him had been correct.

"Stop it, Ann. I can take that from a lot of people but not from you."

Her expression changed and her features registered concern. Momentarily, she dropped her eyes.

"I heard about what happened last night."

"I don't justify my actions to anyone except myself. That's the only person I have to live with."

She gazed at him, and he felt that her eyes were reaching out to him seeking the truth.

"Come out with it. Tell me what is bothering you," he said.

"I have heard a lot of bad things about you, but I have told myself that the people making the statements were on the opposite side. I felt that I knew you better than the others, and that you are trying to build a new life against great odds. But now I wonder whether it was necessary to crush Mr. Starbuck's pride. And was it necessary to beat Lowry so brutally?

The last statement brought a surprised look to Ashton's face.

"I haven't heard anything about Lowry this morning."

"Doctor Henderson said he has a concussion, but doesn't know how serious it is."

"I didn't know that, but believe me, Ann, he brought it on himself."

From her expression, he knew she was not convinced.

"What else is bothering you, Ann?"

"I suppose at times we expect too much from people," she said slowly. "There are qualities in you that are apparent to me. You pride yourself on your integrity and sense of honor, and you have always been extremely kind to me. These things have always impressed me."

She turned and walked around the counter. The morning light from the front window of the store brought out the sheen in her hair. Her long skirt rustled as she walked, and her young, strong figure moved with a natural grace.

"Go on," he said.

"Now I'm beginning to wonder if some of the finer points of your personality aren't being overshadowed by your great desire for power. The importance of winning, at all costs, is evident in your actions."

Ashton studied her as she talked and admired the complete honesty and sincerity in the girl.

"Ann, you only see the end product of a situation, not all the factors that lead up to it. I want to explain a little about what I've done and why.

When I arrived in Summerville, I obviously upset the balance of things."

He spoke slowly and could see that she was trying to understand.

"Starbuck ran this town, the people in it, and the surrounding ranchers. Bullard is king of the mountain and controls through fear what Starbuck doesn't through his economic stranglehold on the community. If I am to exist here, I have to break this circle to survive. And I am going to stay. I'm a threat to both of them, because if I am able to fight them and win, others will do the same."

Ashton walked away from her a few steps and then came back with his thoughts collected.

"It's unfortunate that things turned out as they did in the beginning, but ultimately, I'm sure, I would have clashed with both of them. You are right, I could have kept from driving my cattle across Starbuck's range, but I was mad over being shut out of this town and wanted a showdown with him. I've been fighting for five years, and in that time I have learned a lot about opponents. Some are brave, and some are arrogant cowards. Starbuck has no inner strength, and I knew it. Now, other people know."

She listened attentively to what he said.

"A couple days ago about two hundred rustled cattle ended up on my range in the box canyon area. They came from the Jordan, McGraw, and Michaels ranches as well as from Starbuck's spread. Not only was I stopped from doing business in this town, but someone was trying to discredit me with the other ranchers. Surprisingly, my welcome at the other ranches was good. I explained the situation, and Jordan recommended that we not do anything until we see who makes the first accusation against me. They suspect, as I do, that Starbuck had the cattle planted. I have a few more things to say. Should I go on?'' he asked.

She smiled for the first time and nodded her consent.

"Last night I decided to open up the town as I have opened up Starbuck. I did just that. I would like to be left alone to run my ranch. I'm tired of fighting, and so are my men. But, I won't be pushed anymore. I care about what you think, Ann. I hope you realize that.''

"You can be very convincing,'' she said.

He reached out, took her in his arms, and held her closely. The fragrance from her hair was almost intoxicating to him. She responded, and he felt her shiver. The few moments they held each other seemed like hours, and Ashton felt at peace.

"Please, be careful,'' she murmured.

"When it's over, I hope I have more to offer you than I do now,'' he said.

Outside the store window Pete Brandt had watched for a few minutes and then walked over to the hitch rail, mounted his horse, and rode back to the Owlhoots to report to Jess Bullard. At the same time, Ezra Starbuck and several of his ranch hands rode up to Race Jordan's front porch.

"Ezra,'' Jordan said in acknowledgement. "Get down and sit a spell.''

Starbuck dismounted and walked up the steps of

the ranchhouse, as if he owned it. He was dressed in a grey riding outfit and white Stetson and acted in his usual arrogant manner.

"I came over here to inform you we have a rustler that's moved into our country."

"Is that a fact?" Jordan asked as he smoked his pipe.

"You don't seem very concerned?"

"Well, I am," Jordan said in a strong but quiet voice. His eyes narrowed as he gazed at Starbuck.

"There's thirty or forty head of your cattle and mine and McGraw's and Michaels' over on Ashton's ranch. He's a cattle thief on top of everything else," he said vehemently.

"Who discovered the cattle?"

"One of my men, but that doesn't matter."

Jordan cut him off before he could finish tbe sentences, "But it does matter. Who found the cattle?"

"What's so all-fired important about that," Starbuck shouted. "They're there. That's what counts. We have to ride against Ashton and smash him."

Jordan slowly got up from his chair. The wind blew his white hair, and there was fire in his eyes.

"Don't speak in that tone of voice to me again," he warned.

Starbuck looked at him and knew he had overstepped himself.

"What are we fighting about. One of my riders, Tad Dixon, discovered them."

"What was Dixon doing on Ashton's property?"

For the first time, Starbuck realized something was wrong.

"I told him to scout around over there, and he found them."

"You're a little late in bringing me the information."

"What!" Starbuck said incredulously.

"Ashton was here yesterday. He told me and Charlie and Joe that the cattle had been planted on his property. He offered to bring them back, but I told him not to, that we should wait," Jordan said.

"Wait for what?" Starbuck asked suspiciously.

"To see who brought us the news."

The two men stared at each other. Ford Gentry sat on his horse off to one side and listened to the men. Now, he had a sinking feeling in his stomach. From the beginning, he had thought it strange that Ashton would rustle cattle. Gentry lowered his head and looked at the ground.

"What are you accusing me of," Starbuck yelled.

"Get out of here, Ezra. Don't try to get the rest of us involved in your private feuds."

Red-faced with anger boiling up inside him, Starbuck quickly mounted his horse and rose back towards his ranch with his cowboys trailing behind. Gentry had glanced at Jordan before he rode off, and the ranch owner saw the look of embarrassment on the foreman's face.

"I feel sorry for Gentry. He's a damn good foreman," Jordan said to himself.

9

Couples weaved in and out to the rhythm of the music. Rows of lamps were hung in lines along the interior of the building, accenting the bright colors in the women's dresses. A heavy-set, red-faced man called the turns of a square dance, and the young people seemed not to tire. The building became insufferably hot, and the music, talking, and continual movement of the people added to the general confusion that everyone enjoyed. Homesteaders, cowboys, and townspeople mingled freely. Girls wore bows in their hair, and their faces were flushed with excitement as they danced first with one young man and then another. Punch bowls were in evidence at one end of the long hall, and at the opposite end of the room, a set of benches held several wailing babies.

The men from Ashton's ranch were meeting many new people, especially the girls. Other cowboys were present from the Jordan, McGraw, and Michaels outfits. The young men were scrubbed clean for the first time in weeks. They wore their best boots, gaudy belt buckles, and vests. The lines at the punch bowls were unceasing, and many of the men slipped outside from time to time to dilute their punch drinks with something stronger. Jamie McDonald had Maria Gutierrez as his constant companion, and the two were laughing most of the evening. Older couples lined the walls; the women sitting down and the men discussing cattle and farming.

Ashton had danced several times with Ann Winter and had just poured two fresh glasses of punch. He studied her as her eyes swept the room. Her eyes sparkled and shined in the lamp light. He could tell she was enjoying herself immensely. She wore a long, powder-blue dress that accented her figure. Her long, brown hair swept around her shoulders and framed the smiling face.

He was surprised that many of the townspeople went out of their way to introduce themselves and congratulate him for moving into the area. They felt the impending shift of power and welcomed a man they felt had established himself in the face of great odds.

It was nearly eight in the evening when the Starbuck crew arrived. Caroline Starbuck swept into the hall on the arm of her father. Starbuck's outfit, the largest in the area, trailed behind. Conversation died down as the men viewed one of the most beautiful women they had ever seen. Expressions of envy crossed the faces of the other young women. She was dressed in a gleaming white dress and wore sparkling jewelry. Her long, black hair contrasted brilliantly with her regal costume. Caroline knew the impression she made and carried herself with bearing and pride. She accompanied her father as they spoke with several of the important townspeople and other ranchers.

"She's beautiful, isn't she," Ann said. "You can see how proud her father is."

Ashton was surprised to hear Ann speak so honestly about another woman's beauty, but then he remembered she was without guile.

"Yes, she is," he answered. "But, I happen to like powder-blue dresses."

She smiled up at him, appreciating the gesture.

Ezra Starbuck was proud of his daughter, and it showed. She was his most treasured possession and on her he showered all of his love and affection. On nights like this his pride in his daughter was without rival. The king and his princess moved around the room accepting the homage paid to them. As they passed Ashton, Starbuck did not acknowledge his presence, but his daughter smiled.

Jeff Starbuck suddenly appeared beside Ann.

"May I have this dance," he said in a hesitant manner.

"Why yes, Jeff. I'd like that."

Ashton leaned against the wall and drank his punch slowly. Ann was radiant he thought. The younger Starbuck appeared somewhat clumsy and ill at ease, but Ann smiled at him, and he appeared to gain confidence. Ashton's attention shifted back to Caroline Starbuck. While her father was engrossed in conversation, she slipped away and made her way slowly across the room.

"So we meet again," she said, smiling.

"Hello, Caroline."

"Since you won't ask me to dance, I'll ask you," she said as her eyes sparkled.

"I don't think that would be advisable. Your father might have heart failure."

She laughed and Ashton smiled.

"Where did you get that cut on your face?"

"I fell off a horse."

She gazed at him and her eyes were inviting.

"I wish things were different. There are not many men who interest me," she said in a sincere voice.

"That's a nice thought."

"Don't be surprised if I ride over to see you one of these days."

The preceeding dance had ended, and the room became quieter. Guns were not allowed at the dance, but the cowboys from the various ranches became more tense and uneasy. Ezra Starbuck suddenly realized who his daughter was speaking to and abruptly broke off his conversation and marched across the room.

"Come away from here," Starbuck said in a gruff voice.

He took his daughter by the arm and led her away. The look he gave Ashton was pure hatred. Jamie McDonald walked over and stood by Ashton.

"What was that all about?"

"She was having a little fun at everybody's expense."

"I wish she'd have a little fun at my expense. I've never seen a more beautiful woman," McDonald stated.

Ashton nodded his head in agreement. He looked around for Ann and saw her walking out the door with Jeff Starbuck. The young Starbuck looked uncomfortable and self-conscious as usual. Once outside, he directed Ann to a spot where there was a breeze on the porch.

"You look very beautiful, Ann," he said shyly and dropped his head and looked at the ground.

"Thank you, Jeff. What a nice thing to say."

He fumbled around with his paper and tobacco, attempting to make a cigarette.

"I haven't seen you in town for awhile. Why don't you come in more often," she said while trying to put him at ease.

"I'll do that."

"These dances are enjoyable. I've seen people tonight that I haven't had a chance to talk to in months. It must get lonely out on the range."

"It does," he said succinctly. "I wish I could leave the ranch."

Ann looked around at him.

"It's a beautiful ranch, Jeff."

He glanced at her and said, "Might be if you're a woman."

She understood and was sad.

He was always under pressure from a domineering father whose love was entirely tied up in his beautiful daughter. Jeff was a weak child, and the continual harassment and demands made upon him had not helped him mature into a solid man. Given no real guidance, but much criticism, his outlook on life was not healthy. He hated his father and feared him even more. Life to him was carrying out an endless string of orders. He had long since given up trying to please his father, because the elder Starbuck never appeared to notice when he did a job well and was always quick to criticize him for the slightest mistake. He was a tense, angry young man. He had drifted in with Bullard's group out of desperation. From time to time, he would help the outlaws rustle cattle, take his share of the profits, and feel equal. He knew he was valuable to Bullard, and the outlaw leader treated him like a man.

"Ann, is there a chance for us?" he blurted out.

She was at a loss to answer the question. She wanted to be honest, and yet at the same time she did not want to hurt his feeling.

"Never mind. You answered the question," he said. "It's Ashton isn't it?"

"Yes."

He took a deep breath and exhaled sharply. He looked at her, and the expression on his face was pathetic.

"I guess I just can't win," he said softly.

She put her hands on his arm, but he withdrew quickly.

"Don't feel sorry for me, I couldn't stand that."

He turned quickly and walked into the darkness. She looked after him for several moments and then walked back inside. The music had started again; after a minute, she felt better. Coming towards her with long easy strides was John Ashton, and she was suddenly happy. He was a big, powerful man who moved with confidence and a sense of dignity. His ruggedly handsome face looked down at her, and she was suddenly excited.

The following afternoon Ann was alone in the store checking supplies when Caroline Starbuck entered. Ann's face showed surprise.

"Hi, Caroline. This is a surprise. I hadn't expected to see you in town again so soon."

Caroline Starbuck's mouth formed a small smile, but her eyes did not.

"I had some shopping to do."

"We have some selections of new material. Would you care to see them?"

The two women made small talk while Caroline looked over the new dress-making materials.

"You and John Ashton were together for most of the evening."

"Yes," Ann answered. She smiled as she thought of the previous evening.

"He's an interesting man."

Ann glanced at Caroline with an inquiring look.

"Yes, I think so," Ann replied.

"I don't think my father and John will carry on this feud forever."

"I hope you're right."

"I have a great deal of influence with my father, and I think I can bring the two men together in time. And I like John."

Caroline's obvious attempt to emphasize her familiarity with Ashton slightly irritated Ann, but she did not allow it to show.

"I saw the two of you talking together last night, but I wasn't aware you were friends," Ann said.

Caroline's dark, almost black eyes bore into Ann.

"We have met on the range a few times," she

said, lying.

The effect was what she had hoped for, as she saw Ann's smile fade and a trace of worry cross her face.

"Are you trying to tell me something, Caroline?"

Caroline's eyes flashed and she smiled.

"I just want to make sure you realize it's an open field."

A look of concern clouded Ann's features.

"I realize that I have no hold on him."

"As I said before, I think he is an interesting man," Caroline said in a voice that was almost menacing.

An ominous feeling slowly came over Ann, and she understood why Caroline Starbuck was there.

"You're trying to warn me, aren't you, Caroline, that you intend to actively pursue John."

Caroline flashed a quick look at Ann.

"Yes. I think he could be a very powerful man in the territory."

Ann was silent for a moment as she considered the statement.

"I think you are wrong if you believe he is after power. He wants to be left alone to run his ranch."

Caroline put down the material she was holding. "He has many of the same qualities my father has."

"John is a lonely man and tired of fightin," Ann said. "He has been forced to protect himself from a hostile country, but I do not believe he wants to rule this range or any other. He just wants to be left alone."

"I don't think you know men that well," Caroline replied. "They continually seek power. It's their nature to want to become powerful, to control. I want that type of man."

"Don't you think that part of it is wanting something or someone that you can't have?"

Caroline became visibly angry. "I've always been able to get any man I wanted."

"You don't need to convince me of that. You and I grew up in this country together. I've seen what you have done to one man after another. But John Ashton is different."

Caroline's eyes blazed as she declared, "I can have him, too."

"Thanks for the warning. That's really why you came here today, wasn't it?"

"I came here to look at dress material, but you don't have anything that suits me."

"Caroline, I sincerely hope you are able to get your father and John Ashton to quit fighting, but I don't think you will be able to. I certainly hope you don't do anything rash that will worsen the situation."

Caroline was furious. "What I do is none of your business."

She turned and left the store without looking back.

Down the street Sheriff Jim Mayberry had been sitting behind his desk studying wanted posters when Ezra Starbuck entered. Starbuck walked over to a large chair in his usual arrogant manner and seated himself. His mannerisms indicated that it was beneath his dignity to be in the ramshackled office.

"Morning, Ezra."

"I thought we should talk," Starbuck said without bothering to acknowledge the greeting.

Mayberry studied the rancher. He expected trouble and had been waiting for Starbuck's visit which he knew would come. In a way, he welcomed the confrontation. It was time for plain talk.

"What's on you mind, Ezra?"

"Why didn't you jail Ashton the other night when he beat up Lowry?" Starbuck asked in a loud voice.

"He didn't break any law as far as I know. Lowry was fixing to catch him in a cross-fire, and it didn't work. Can't blame Ashton much for knocking a little sense into Lowry. He ain't too well yet. Took a bad beating."

"You should have jailed Ashton for assault."

Mayberry's eyes narrowed as he spoke. "The charge wouldn't have stuck. Lowry tried to pull a gun on Ashton."

"I'm not interested in the details. The point is that Ashton should be behind bars. The Town Council hired you to see that law and order is upheld in this town. Ashton is dangerous and a threat to the community."

Mayberry said nothing.

"There's another thing that's bothering me, Jim. Ashton and his men forced their way into my hotel and made my manager give them rooms. That's a violation of another law, trespassing probably."

Mayberry slowly lit his Pipe and drew the smoke deep into his lungs.

"He paid for the rooms, didn't he?"

The anger was evident on Stabuck's face. "I don't care about that. He was on my premises illegally, and I want you to arrest him," he shouted.

"This conversation is long overdue," Mayberry replied. "Let's get a few things straight. The Town Council hired me, but you control that council completely. Those men vote the way you tell them to do. I was hired to keep law and order in this town, and that I have done."

Starbuck attempted to interrupt Mayberry: "I think that . . . "

"Just wait until I've finished my say," the Sheriff said in a firm voice.

The look of determination on Mayberry's face caused Starbuck to remain silent.

"The people of this town are safe to walk the streets, and the few times I have had to arrest someone, the law was served. There was never any criticism of the way I handled things until Ashton came along. He's not the type of man to fool around with. You learned that. I've carried out your orders and seen that this town is a safe place to live in. That's what I was hired to do and I've done it. But I won't play the fool for anyone, and that includes you. I don't like the thought of trying to arrest Ashton on some trumped-up charge. He won't let anyone make him play the fool. And if you're thinking about having me get shot in the line of duty so you can bring federal marshals against him, you can forget it. I don't get shot for anyone."

Starbuck stared at the Sheriff and was barely able to contain the fury that lay below the surface.

"I think you have lost your nerve."

"It's not a question of nerve. It's a question of what is right."

Starbuck rose from the chair.

"There's not much else that we have to talk about. At a special meeting this afternoon the Town Council will vote to remove you as sheriff and put in a new man."

"Mind telling me who's taking my place?"

Starbuck thought for a moment in his perverse manner and then looked at Mayberry and smiled. "Ringo Vermillion," Starbuck said.

Mayberry's face showed both surprise and disgust.

"Starbuck, you can't be serious."

The rancher was enjoying the conversation now, and it pleased him that Mayberry was upset.

"I assure you that I am serious. He has already been sent for."

The Sheriff rose behind his desk, and his anger was something Starbuck had never seen.

"That man is nothing but a hired killer. Whoever hires him does so for one reason and one reason alone—he wants someone murdered. Vermillion stinks of death, and it follows him wherever he goes," Mayberry said in an emotion-filled voice.

Starbuck was unmoved by Mayberry's outrage.

"At least he will be able to uphold the law. He's afraid of no man."

Mayberry had all he could do to contain himself.

"Vermillion doesn't even know what law is. I've seen him before. He's a sick man. You can see it in his eyes. He enjoys killing. Ezra, you wanted law in this town and you've had it. If you bring Vermillion in here, you will destroy law and order."

"I want him here in this town waiting for Ashton. I want Ashton to have time to think about what is in store for him."

The startled expression had not left Mayberry's face.

"I don't think you could legally let that man wear a star. Certainly, no court would ever upbold anything that Vermillion does."

Starbuck smiled. "No court is going to have to pass on his actions."

"I see your game. Vermillion always calls a man out. The man either has to face him and fight, or be branded a coward. You know that Ashton is no coward and figure he'll die in the gunfight."

"You're smart, Mayberry. Too bad you wouldn't follow my orders."

Mayberry shook his head in wonderment, and an expression of loathing crossed his face.

"Starbuck, I think you're as sick as Vermillion. Now, get out of my office. I'm still Sheriff until the council meets."

The rancher flashed a look of hatred at the Sheriff and left the building.

10

Ezra Starbuck stood on his front porch watching the two riders approach. It had taken three weeks for Vermillion to arrive from the Mexican border town where he lived when he wasn't working. His ranch hand had gone into town to bring the new Sheriff to Starbuck's ranch for a talk.

He watched Ringo Vermillion dismount. Starbuck could not discern what his age might be, but he guessed him to be in his early thirties. The two men shook hands without speaking as they appraised each other. Once they were inside Starbuck's office, the rancher was able to study the gunman.

Vermillion was dressed in black clothing, wore a black hat, and carried a silver-colored revolver slung low in a shiny black holster. He was slightly shorter than normal height and was extremely thin. He wore his yellow hair long down to the shoulders, but what caught Starbuck's attention were his facial features. His face was pale and the white skin stretched tightly against the bone structure, giving him an almost skeletal appearance. He had thin lips and a nose that was flat against his face. The wide nostrils added to the mask-like appearance. His eyes were cold, expressionless and the lightest blue that Starbuck had ever seen. Now, they were fixed on the rancher and did not waver.

"Drink?" Starbuck asked, and motioned for Vermillion to take a chair opposite his desk.

"Yes," he answered and sat down.

"You were quite a while in coming," the rancher observed as he handed the gunman a glass of whiskey.

"I had some unfinished business to take care of," Vermillion said in a soft, strained voice. His eyes never left Starbuck, nor did his expression change.

"I made arrangements for you to stay in the best suite at the hotel. All your meals and bar expenses will be picked up."

Vermillion just nodded. His unchanging stare was beginning to make the rancher feel uncomfortable. The killer handed his glass back to Starbuck for a refill. He then drained the second glass, and Starbuck realized that his eyes hardly ever blinked.

"You found your office, the Sheriff's office?"

"Yes."

"I suppose we should get down to business," Starbuck said.

"Whenever you are ready."

"I've hired you to kill a man. John Ashton is his name, and he's a rancher near here."

"Tell me about him," Vermillion said in his soft voice.

"He's not a gunman, but he is good with a gun. He killed one man with a handgun in a fight and another two men with a shotgun in town. He's not particularly fast, but he is tough."

"What is his background?"

"From what I have learned, he was a Major in the Confederate Cavalry. He had extensive battle experience and a good record."

Vermillion was silent as he digested the information. "Do you care how or when he dies?"

"No. I just want him dead. He comes into this country and thinks he can run it. I want him gone or dead, and I don't think he will leave."

Starbuck considered his previous statements and was surprised that ordering a man killed did not bother him anymore.

"The price is two thousand dollars," Vermillion said in his soft, grating voice.

A look of irritation spread over the rancher's face.

"Wait a minute. We agreed on one thousand."

"We didn't agree on anything. You sent a man to see me with two hundred and said you were willing to pay one thousand. We never talked before, or you would realize that I set the price."

"One thousand is a reasonable price," Starbuck said in a loud, agitated voice.

"I don't bargain. Two thousand, take it or leave it."

Starbuck stared at the gunman. Vermillion returned the gaze and his expression remained flat, unemotional. After looking at the ranch and learning that Starbuck controlled the town, he felt confident that his two-thousand-dollar demand would be met.

"Alright," Starbuck said grudgingly, knowing

he was beaten.

"Have another eight hundred delivered to me in town tomorrow."

"It will be at least two days before I can get the money from the bank in Desert City."

"Two days, then," Vermillion replied.

The rancher studied the gunman wondering if he was as brutal as his reputation made him out to be. The small body, ugly face, and deceivingly soft voice were not confidence-builders.

"Do you mind if I ask you a question?" Starbuck asked.

"No."

"How many men have you killed?"

"Twenty-six," he answered quietly as his translucent eyes remained fixed on Starbuck.

As Jim Mayberry rode up to the Ashton ranch he was surprised at how much progress had been made in construction of the ranch house, corrals, bunkhouses, barn, and other buildings. The buildings were well constructed, built to last, and pride of workmanship was evident. Mexican laborers were everywhere, unloading supplies and lumber, working on the roofs of buildings and generally busy at a dozen different jobs.

He noticed that the general tenor of activity was harmonious, and he realized that the laborers were enjoying the job and wanted to please. Mexicans worked side by side with cowboys, and the general atmosphere was one of equality, far different from what it was in town, where the Mexicans were shoved aside into their own little community.

On the front porch leaning over a table covered

with drawing and sketches were Ashton, Ben Mathews, and Jamie McDonald. They straightened up as Mayberry approached.

"Welcome, Sheriff. Get down and join us," Ashton said.

"Thanks," Mayberry replied. He dismounted and tied his horse to the hitchrail.

"Quite impressive," Mayberry said as he looked out over the nearly completed ranch quarters.

"I'm satisfied with the progress. The men had done a good job."

Mayberry nodded his head in approval. "I don't mind telling you. It appears to be the most impressive ranch around."

Mayberry exchanged greetings with the other men.

"Did you just come over here for the ride?" Ashton asked.

Mayberry took a deep breath and exhaled sharply. His eyes narrowed as he looked at Ashton. "I wish it was that simple."

Ashton leveled his full attention on Mayberry, and the ex-Sheriff realized that he possessed one supreme quality: unquestioned strength. Mathews and McDonald had their attention fully fixed on Ashton. They depend on him, he thought.

"First of all, I'm no longer Sheriff. The Town Council fired me."

"I heard that rumor."

Mayberry shifted his stance. "I waited a few weeks before coming out here. Didn't know if Starbuck would go through with his threat. But today I found out he meant it."

"Go on," Ashton said quietly.

"I was fired for not going up against you. Starbuck wants you dead. I guess there's nothing that can stop his hatred. Anyway, they've employed a new Sheriff by the name of Ringo Vermillion. He hit town today. Ringo is a hired killer, and his one and only job is to kill you."

"So, it's to be a bottom-of-the-deck deal," Ashton stated.

"Yes. Starbuck must have paid plenty to get him here. He only hires out for big money, does his job, and leaves. He's killed a couple of dozen, all in the same way. He finds them, and then makes them fight or turn tail and run. The lucky ones run; the others are all dead."

Ashton nodded his head in understanding. His discipline was his strength. He had been taught to make his own decisions at an early age, and now in his mind he was deciding what to do. Men placed their faith and trust in him to make the correct decisions, and his men were looking to him now. Being the leader, Ashton had nowhere to turn. The ultimate decision was his alone. This was the way it had always been in combat. It was his part to play.

Mayberry continued talking, "He'll just sit there and wait for you. He knows you have to come and meet him or lose face. His plan is simple, and it works well."

"I'm not running," Ashton said in an even voice that rang of finality. "Starbuck must be desperate, if he had to go this far."

McDonald spoke up for the first time, "It wouldn't be hard for us to catch this fellow and hang him."

"No," Ashton said. "First, that would be murdering a man with a star. And second, I don't play the game that way."

"Better to be alive than dead, John," Mathews interjected.

Ashton grinned. "I want to thank you all for the faith you have in my shooting ability."

"He's a sick-looking man on the inside as well as on the outside," Mayberry explained. "Vermillion is not an albino, but close to it. His face looks like a skull with skin stretched over it, and he has these light blue eyes that you can almost see through to the back of his head. The man smells of death, and he doesn't act like a normal person."

"What else do you know about him?" Ashton asked. His face showed no fear, and he still stood in the same, confident manner as when Mayberry arrived.

"He practices with a revolver every day and must shoot fifty rounds or more. Today he was out behind Mexican town practicing drawing and firing over and over again. He's unbelievably fast on the draw: smooth, confident, and accurate. You know, I have been Sheriff in a number of towns and have seen a lot of gunmen. Vermillion is the best."

"Does he ever use any other weapon?"

"No. His weapon is a silver-plated Colt .44 with an ivory handle. It's his trademark. I've never heard of him using another weapon."

113

Ashton glanced at his men and then back at Mayberry. "Will you do me a favor?"

"Anything I can," Mayberry replied.

"Spread the word that I will meet him in town Saturday afternoon."

Mayberry stared at him. "You sure you know what you're doing?"

"I'm sure. Let it be known that I will face him alone."

Mathews took a step forward. He was angry. His face showed it, but Ashton held up his hand, and his foreman remained quiet.

"I want to thank you for the information, Jim. You've been a great help. I know you lost your job because of me, and I appreciate what you have done."

"I wish I could be of more help. I will pass on the information."

A few minutes later Mayberry rode off, and Ashton turned to face his two men. Mathews was furious, his face was red, and he appeared ready to explode.

"Starbuck is a coward, and this is just his underhanded way to get you killed. You don't have anything to prove, John. You've taken everything this country had handed to you and have beaten them. It's senseless to go against a hired killer," Mathews declared.

"I don't run and hide from any man."

"That's not the point. Why risk everything by going against a professional gunman. There's nothing fair about the way they fight. It's foolish courage to go against a killer, and I don't want to

114

see you die to prove a point," Mathews said in a loud voice.

Ashton was touched by Mathews' concern and grinned. "Don't count me out, Ben. You haven't even heard my plan yet."

Jamie McDonald spoke up for the first time, "I could drop him with a rifle. If he's a hired gunman, he doesn't deserve better. It'd be like killing a mad dog."

"No. We'll do it my way. Here's what I have in mind."

It was nearly noon on Saturday when Ezra Starbuck and his riders entered Summerville and put up their horses at the livery stable. As usual, he was dressed in a fashionable grey suit and stetson and looked and acted like the powerful rancher he was. Starbuck and Ford Gentry took the lead and strolled along the boardwalk towards the saloon. The small town was filling fast as cowboys and homesteaders from miles around came to watch the main attraction.

As he walked along, Starbuck tipped his hat to several ladies, but all the men were forced to step aside in deference to his position. On the other side of the street, he could see men pointing at him and talking rapidly.

Starbuck smiled. They will soon learn again who runs this country, he thought. The thought of Ashton meeting Vermillion in a gunfight before the entire community pleased him. The contingent reached the saloon, where a loud outpouring of noise marked the center of activity in town. Cowboys stood in small groups around the entrance to the bar. Inside, the drinking activity and loud voices had reached a peak, and several bartenders were working at full speed to quench the insatiable thirsts of the patrons.

Starbuck hit the swinging doors with his hands, and they struck the men just inside the room. Angry at first, the men stopped talking and stepped aside as Starbuck entered. The talk quieted noticeably, and Starbuck was again pleased that he was the center of attention. Most of the men had their attention riveted on the rancher. In his self-assured manner, Starbuck slowly looked around the room and finally picked out Bake Lowry seated at a table.

"You boys have a few drinks on me," Starbuck said to his cowboys.

He walked across the room to Lowry's table, and conversation began again in the bar.

"Bake, how are you feeling?" Starbuck asked.

Lowry did not look healthy. He had lost weight and was still feeling the effects of the beating Ashton had administered. His face was pale, and the impassive look of confidence was missing.

"I'm fine, Ezra, and you?"

"Feel wonderful. Couldn't be better," Starbuck announced and seated himself at the table. "How's our new Sheriff doing?"

"He'll be here in a few minutes. He doesn't alter his schedule much. He does the same things at the same time every day. He doesn't talk to anybody unless they speak first. And not many people talk to him. He looks like death on two legs. Strangest

116

man I've ever seen, and I been in this business a lot of years.''

"Any problems with him?" the rancher asked.

"Naw. He keeps to himself. Leaves the hotel late in the morning, goes back yonder by Mexican town, practices his drawing and shooting, and comes here for a drink or two to play solitaire. Then he goes back to the hotel, eats again, and doesn't leave his room until the middle of the evening. He plays poker until midnight and then prowls around the streets. Nobody goes out at night with him around.''

Starbuck smiled.

"He is just the man I want for this job.''

Lowry looked skeptical.

"I hope he leaves after he kills Ashton. Eventually, Vermillion could be trouble if he decided to stay. The townspeople are upset enough just having to look at him for a few days,'' Lowry noted.

"He'll be gone tomorrow,'' Starbuck said.

"Those eyes of his are strange. They look right through you. It's hard to know if he's focusing on something or just looking into space. He doesn't care for women. The only human thing about him is his poker playing. He's not that good, but he usually wins, because nobody will bluff him. I've seen men throw in some good hands just because they were winning too much from him. He hasn't helped business.''

"You seem to be doing an enormous volume this afternoon.''

"Yeah. But it'll only last one day. After the killing, the town will be empty again. By the way, what if Ashton should win?''

"There's no chance of that. I don't think there is a man alive that can match Vermillion's speed.''

"That's the talk around, alright,'' Lowry acknowledged.

Talk in the saloon suddenly came to an abrupt stop. Every eye turned toward the door as Vermillion entered. He slowly looked around the room, and the cowboys shifted their eyes towards the floor or off to one side as Vermillion's gaze passed them. Satisfied that there was no challenge to him, the gunfighter moved leisurely across the room to the table where Lowry and Starbuck sat. Again, Starbuck was reminded that Vermillion's face resembled a skeleton with skin stretched across it. There was no hint of emotion or recognition on Vermillion's face as he neared the table.

"Ringo, how are you?'' Starbuck asked.

"Fine,'' Vermillion answered in his soft voice. "Do you have the rest of the money?''

"Yes. You will be paid in full as soon as it is over.''

"You are sure this man, Ashton, will be here this afternoon?'' the gunman asked.

"He sent word that he would be here, and that means you will meet him this afternoon.''

Starbuck suddenly realized another strange thing about the gunfighter. His eyes didn't blink. The thought made him momentarily uneasy.

"He has some plan in mind,'' Vermillion said.

"What do you mean?'' Starbuck asked.

"He says he will be here, and you believe him. You hate him and fear him, yet you know be is a

118

man of his word. He has picked the time and place, so he has a plan," Vermillion said in his slow, almost hoarse voice.

Starbuck's face reddened, but he said nothing.

Lowry watched the two men and was amused. Not dumb, he thought to himself, not dumb at all.

"Station your men along the street to neutralize anyone that Ashton may bring with him," Vermillion said.

Starbuck nodded his consent.

"He's coming in now," one of the cowboys near the door shouted.

The saloon grew loud with excitement as most of the men started talking at the same time. The doorway was crowded, and the men standing in the rear attempted to look over the heads of the front row of cowboys.

Starbuck got up from the chair and looked through one of the small front windows. He recognized Ashton, Ben Mathews, and Jamie McDonald as they slowly rode up the street. The rancher smiled as he viewed Ashton. As he studied his enemy, Starbuck recognized a character trait that he thought spelled doom for Ashton. He has an intense sense of honor that will not allow him to move away from danger.

Starbuck grudgingly felt admiration for Ashton, but his realization that only one of them could be the recognized leader in the community overcame any thoughts of fair play. Beneath Ashton's self-sufficiency, he recognized a personality flaw that would kill him. For all his tough exterior character and impregnable shell, Ashton had very real inner feelings that were too human, too aligned with a sense of fair play. Starbuck knew that he, himself, was not troubled with the same problem.

Ashton and his men rode slowly westward on the main street. The sun was starting to sink in the sky, and the buildings were beginning to cast longer shadows. The three men were all concentrating on the sun's position, although their eyes were fixed straight ahead.

"How much more time?" Mathews asked as the men dismounted in front of Thurman Winter's store.

"About a half an hour should be right," Ashton replied. "Let's get on down the street to the saloon."

They walked three abreast as they advanced. Men stepped aside as the contingent moved at a steady pace toward Lowry's. Mathews and McDonald were watchful, and their eyes moved over each man they approached. All three men wore revolvers, and McDonald carried his rifle in a cocked position ready to fire.

After they reached the front of the saloon, the men inside moved backward away from the door and formed a passageway. Ashton walked casually among the cowhands in a deliberate yet unhurried manner. His eyes surveyed the room and immediately rested on the table where Vermillion and Starbuck were seated.

Ashton and Vermillion studied each other. The saloon was completely quiet. The onlookers did not shuffle their feet, cough, clear their throats, or clink their glasses. It was a time when the full attention of every man was occupied with the

120

scene unfolding before them.

The absolute quiet was broken by Ashton's heavy footsteps as he walked across the room and stood before the poker table.

Vermillion's expression had not changed. His pale eyes met Ashton's penetrating stare and held. Starbuck's eyes were hooded, as if he was aloof from the confrontation, but a slight smile spread across his features. Starbuck searched Ashton's face for some sign of fear or uneasiness. He found none.

"The street will be a good place to meet in half an hour," Ashton announced in a loud voice.

Vermillion did not reply, and his pale eyes did not move from Ashton's face.

"It will be just you and me. My men have been instructed to stay out of it," Ashton said in a steady voice.

"Alright," Vermillion replied softly.

Ashton's attention turned to Starbuck.

"You are a gutless snake. I have no respect for a man who hides behind a hired gun," Ashton said in a flat voice.

Starbuck's face turned red, and he sputtered and started to stand.

"No man talks to me that way," Starbuck shouted.

"I just did," Ashton said and smiled.

"Your time is about over. Ashton, you only have a little time to live. Enjoy it," Starbuck yelled.

Suddenly, it dawned upon Starbuck that he was being baited. Ashton was attempting to draw him into a confrontation before he met Vermillion. He suddenly sat down and was quiet.

Seeing that he would get no more response from Starbuck, Ashton turned and walked out of the bar. Mathews and McDonald followed him.

Starbuck glanced around the room and saw the expressions of contempt on many of the cowboys' faces. He had lost the respect of some, he thought, but he would rule unchallenged again when Ashton was dead.

Ashton and his men walked westward along the street.

"I want to talk with Ann for a few minutes."

"Where are you going to stand?" McDonald asked.

The men stopped walking, and Ashton carefully studied the street and the distances between buildings.

"I think in front of the print shop," Ashton stated.

"Good spot. I was thinking that's about the right distance, seventy-five to eighty yards," McDonald said.

"I still don't think you ought to be doing this," Mathews stressed.

"Too late now, Ben. Find yourselves good spots to watch the show, and keep your eyes on Starbuck," Ashton told them before walking into Winter's store.

His men watched him walk away. Mathews looked at McDonald with an air of concern.

"Just between you and me, if John loses, I want to shoot that black snake of a killer," Mathews said in a low voice.

"Ben, I already had that thought in my mind," McDonald said as he tapped his rifle.

Inside the shop, talk ceased as Ashton entered. Several women stared at him briefly and left the store. Ann Winter was folding a garment behind the counter, and her motions stopped suddenly.

"For awhile, I wondered whether you would come."

Ashton did not reply. He walked slowly across the room and stopped in front of her. The longing was in him along with the fear he might lose her.

"You knew I would come," he said.

Her eyes held his, and her thoughts penetrated his awareness. He dropped his eyes.

"A man has to move forward, always forward," he said slowly. "The past is dead to me. There is nothing left in the South. You can't go back to nothing. I'm staking everything on today and the future."

"John, it doesn't have to be this way. There is no reason why you have to fight that pathetic little man. What makes you risk everything we might have in the future just to prove a point?"

Ashton shifted his weight from one foot to the other.

"What drives a man is hard to explain. If you want success bad enough, it drives you and will never let you go. You will pay whatever price is necessary to gain it."

"It's more than that isn't it, John? It's pride that forces you to go out there."

She shook her head slowly from side to side.

"It isn't worth it," she said and he could see the

pleading look in her eyes.

"There is no other road left open to me."

She reached out and touched his arm with her hand.

"It's too bad that you can depend on nobody but yourself. Not me, not anyone. I would have thought better of you." Her words stung him and cut deeper than any confrontation with his adversaries. The reproof was direct and unrelenting.

"You have learned too much of the cruelties of men," she said. "You have fought too much, too often. How can I penetrate that steel will? Must it always be like this between us?".

"Men and women had a difficult time understanding each other," he said.

"I don't want you to risk your life out there, John."

He rested his hands lightly on her shoulders. He could feel her body tremble, and she dropped her head to hide the emotion.

"The challenge was made, and I have to accept it. It won't always be like this."

Ann brought her head upward in a sharp motion, and her eyes blazed.

"Oh yes it will. Ever since you came to this country you have had to fight one battle after another. They won't leave you alone until they kill you, or you them. You can't go on living this way. I know I can't. I don't want to have to worry every day that you may be killed."

The silence hung between them.

"Ann, I don't know what else to say to you."

"Well, then don't talk," she said and threw her

124

arms around him.

His strong arms held her tightly, but the feeling of cold fear and impending doom stayed within her.

"I don't intend to die out there. Just hold on for a little longer," he said reassuringly.

Five minutes later he left the store and stood at the edge of the boardwalk looking eastward towards the saloon. He surveyed the town, and his senses were totally sharp and alert. He felt free and the excitement surged through him. It was the same feeling that had swept over him numerous times before the cavalry battles. At the same time he felt the loneliness, the solitude of standing alone before the ultimate test.

His mind traveled to the bystanders lining the street. The smell of death was in the air. He wondered at the perverse side of man that drew human beings, like wolves, to the kill. The scent of death draws them and holds them like no other emotion, he thought.

The showdown was here, and Ashton welcomed it. He intended to destroy the deadlock and Starbuck's hold on the town. The thought of possibly dying did not enter his mind. Only defeat and losing were unacceptable.

He looked at the sun as it continued to descend in the west, and the afternoon temperature grew cooler. Along the boardwalks he could hear the low, confused, indistinct conversations of the cowboys and homesteaders. The uneasiness of the bystanders was apparent. They were drawn like moths to a flame, but they did not want to get too

125

close.

Ashton's senses of smell, sight, and touch were intensified as he stepped out into the street and slowly walked to a position across from the printer's shop. His body reacted to the pressure, and the impressions that swept before his eyes were clear and sharp. His eyes marked each man who moved, and the picture was complete in his mind.

In his right hand, he held a new Winchester .44 rifle, cocked and ready to fire. The sights had been calibrated for eighty yards. He stood with his feet spread slightly, most of his weight on his right leg. He rested his left hand on his hip. The rifle in his right hand pointed straight at the ground.

The murmur from the crowd picked up as the seconds ticked away. The sun was directly over Ashton's shoulders, casting a long shadow out in front of him.

All conversation suddenly ceased as Vermillion emerged from the saloon and stepped into the dusty street. The men viewing the scene hardly breathed. Nobody wanted to draw attention to himself by making any kind of a movement.

Vermillion looked around him and for a few moments studied the men standing along the street. Then he began to walk slowly towards Ashton. Ringo Vermillion had walked towards men many times before. They always died. He had little human emotion in him, and no feelings for the men he killed. Ashton was just another man that stood in his way, an obstacle to be swept aside. He had long since quit trying to prove who was the better man. Now it was a well-paying job.

126

Ashton straightened his stance and waited until Vermillion reached the imaginary point eighty yards away from him. In one smooth movement, he raised the rifle and fired. The slug splattered dust in front of Vermillion, and the surprised gunman stopped walking.

"That's far enough, Vermillion," Ashton said in a loud voice.

He worked the lever-action rifle in a swift motion, and the weapon was again ready to fire.

Vermillion was momentarily confused. The distance was too great for accuracy in a showdown gunfight using revolvers. He squinted his eyes trying to read the expression on Ashton's face, but the sun's rays were directly in his eyes, and Ashton was an obscure, vague man in the distance. He realized that he had been tricked.

"Vermillion, make your play or get out of town."

The insult stung the thin man. For once, his eyes showed emotion—hatred.

"You've been paid to fight. Have you lost your guts?"

Ashton's challenge tore at Vermillion. Throwing caution aside, he drew his revolver in a lightning-fast movement, and then thumbed back the hammer. His body was bent slightly in a gunfighter's crouch. The Colt .44 roared and bucked in his hand.

At the first indication of movement by Vermillion, Ashton jumped to the right and landed on his right knee, in a crouched position. Simultaneously, the butt of the rifle jammed into his shoulder and the smooth wood of the rifle stock touched his face. Sighting of the rifle and squeezing of the trigger were done automatically as he had done hundreds of times in the past. The blast from the rifle echoed off the fronts of the building.

Vermillion's bullet grazed Ashton's left shoulder and threw his body slightly to the left. But Ashton's eyes never left the gunman.

The rifle slug tore into Vermillion's chest. His arms were thrown in the air, and the mouth opened wide as he was tossed backward onto the ground. As he was being propelled backward, his revolver fired a second time, but the shot was straight up into the air. When he struck the ground, the impact made his head bounce in the dust. The gunman groaned softly, flinched, and lay still.

Oblivious to the slight wound, Ashton levered another round into the rifle's chamber and slowly stood up.

"Did you see that?" one of the cowboys shouted.

Several of the cowboys let out yells, and the men began moving and talking.

Ashton advanced down the middle of the street in unhurried strides. He stopped in front of Vermillion's lifeless body, picked up the dead gunman's revolver, and looked about him searching the crowd with his eyes.

Starbuck stood in front of the saloon, his face contorted with rage. Ford Gentry stood next to him.

"That damn fool. Why didn't he walk closer," Starbuck exclaimed to his foreman.

Ashton picked Starbuck out of the crowd of men and walked towards him. As Ashton drew closer, the men around Starbuck and Gentry fell back and were quiet. Starbuck suddenly felt fear grip him, and his face turned pale.

Ashton stepped on to the boardwalk and stopped two feet away from Starbuck. With a swift motion, Ashton hurled the dead gunman's revolver at Starbuck's stomach. The heavy gun struck the rancher and dropped to the wooden walk. Starbuck grunted, and his eyes went wide with fear.

"Here. You paid for this job. Pick it up and do it yourself, if you have any courage," Ashton said in a hard voice.

Starbuck was speechless. He turned around, walked swiftly to his horse, mounted, and rode out of town without looking back.

Gentry took a deep breath, exhaled sharply, and slowly walked to his horse.

A crowd had formed around the dead gunman. Men were pushing in as close as they could to get a look at him. The sight angered Ashton, and he turned and walked toward the hotel with Mathews and McDonald. Although none of the men he passed attempted to stop him, more than a few congratulated him.

The trio entered the hotel, and a look of dread flashed across the clerk's face. He had the room keys on the counter before Ashton reached it.

"Have three meals and a bottle of whiskey sent up to my room," Ashton told him.

Mathews had already summonded the doctor

who arrived a few minutes later with his black bag. He treated the slight arm wound and departed.

Jim Mayberry was the next visitor. He grinned as he looked at Ashton.

"I thought you might like to know that a few minutes ago the Town Council offered me my old job back. I took it and a raise in salary too," he said and smiled. "They didn't even bother to consult Starbuck."

11

After leaving town, Ezra Starbuck rode back to his ranch and locked himself in his study. He opened a bottle of whiskey and downed one glass after another, although the alcohol did not have much effect on the brooding rancher. His outward condition was disheveled, but he was alert. The one extraordinary feature about the man at that moment was his eyes, which were bloodshot and sunken.

Two hours later he sent for Ford Gentry. The foreman carefully scrutinized his employer but said nothing.

"I'm putting and end to him once and for all," Starbuck announced in a voice tinged with bitterness.

Gentry shook his head slowly from side to side.

"Ezra, why don't we quit this darned fighting."

Starbuck's eyes blazed in the lamplight.

"Quit! I won't quit until he's dead," he shouted.

"It's not getting us anywhere, and the country is slowly turning against us," the foreman said quietly.

"Hang the country. Hang them all. I don't care what they think," he yelled.

Starbuck was now breathing hard; his chest

heaved in and out.

"There is plenty of room for all of us to live in peace. This fighting is getting us nowhere."

Starbuck got up from the chair, put his fists on the desk in front of him, and leaned forward.

"There's not room for the two of us," he said passionately. "There never will be."

Gentry was silent. Starbuck's irrational behavior worried him, and he thought of seeking Doctor Henderson's help.

"Are you listening to me, Ford?"

Gentry nodded.

"I can't find my son, my worthless son, so I want you to ride out to the Owlhoots and contact Jess Bullard. I want as many men as he can get to join forces with us to burn out Ashton and his crew," the rancher announced.

Gentry was flabbergasted, and his face showed astonishment.

"Ezra, you can't be serious."

"Can't be. Can't be you say. Well, I am," he yelled.

Gentry thought Starbuck was on the verge of collapse. Starbuck's movements were erratic, and his wild-eyed look was frightening.

"Doing something like that would bring the U. S. Marshalls down on us in a hurry. They won't stand for range war, even in this wild country."

"I don't care what happens afterwards. I want Ashton dead, do you hear me?"

"I won't do it," Gentry said emphatically.

"What do you mean you won't do it. You're my foreman. You'll do anything I tell you."

132

Gentry's eyes narrowed and his stare held Starbuck's eyes. In years past, Starbuck had often been brash, tactless, and impolite in his arrogant ways, but he had always treated his foreman with a certain amount of deference and was civil with him at all times. He knew that Gentry held the ranch together and was the heart of the huge operation.

"Don't talk to me in that tone of voice, Ezra."

"Why won't you do what I tell you?"

"Because it's wrong."

"That man has brought shame on this ranch. Can't you see that?"

"I've seen a lot of things lately that I don't like."

"What do you mean by that?"

"Somebody planted stolen cattle on Ashton's range. A gunfighter was hired to kill him. Now, you want to join forces with a bunch of outlaws to burn out his spread. Hell, Ezra, what is this ranch becoming?"

"Ford, I'm ordering you to ride out there and meet with Bullard."

Gentry shook his head in a negative way.

"I helped you build this ranch. We fought Indians together. We hunted down rustlers and kept back anybody who tried to take this range. I've still got lead in me to prove that I worked hard for you. But there is one thing I won't do for you, and that is ride with outlaws. Once you cross that line, you are no better than they are," Gentry emphasized.

"Then you are through here," Starbuck said in a bitter voice. "You've lost your guts."

Gentry was on the verge of saying something but

133

stopped himself.

"I'll let that pass. Think about what you are doing Ezra. A move like that will destroy you and this ranch."

"Get out."

Gentry left the house and walked out into the cool night air. He had been the backbone of the ranch for more than twenty years, exerting a dominate influence on the owner, making a majority of the decisions, leading the men with a forceful yet quiet personality, meeting hardship and tribulation with an unyielding strength. He even played a major role in raising the children. The Starbuck Ranch was the product of Ford Gentry's life, yet he was never jealous of the owner, never resented the fact that the ranch could not have been built into a minor empire without his influence and foresight. However, like so many men of the era, he held steadfast to the Victorian principles of loyalty and honor. Even now, his brooding concern was for the well-being of Starbuck and the ranch. He feared that Starbuck was losing control.

Gentry walked slowly toward the corral. For the first time in twenty years I don't know where I'll sleep, he thought.

Ashton surveyed his ranch from a rise in the foothills at the base of the Owlhoot mountain range. The buildings looked like a small settlement from a distance, and he smiled from a feeling of pride and ownership. The Mexican laborers were finishing the last of the construction work and would be heading back to Summerville in a few days. He would miss their pleasant chatter, guitar-playing, and singing in the evenings. One of the men, a portly, good-natured worker had been doing the cooking for the work crews and had agreed to stay on as the ranch cook. The Mexican variety of cooking was different for the men at first, but now they liked it and Raul Hernandez was now the pride of the outfit.

In the background the cattle could be seen dotting the prairie for as far as the eye could see. Ashton turned in the saddle as he sensed rather than saw a rider approaching out of the foothills. The rider was mounted on a mule and was leading a pack horse. The man also stopped and inspected Ashton. He carried a Henry .44 rifle like many Ashton had seen and used in the war. From his alert manner, Ashton surmised that he expected trouble.

Ashton smiled and waved to put the man at ease. As the rider came forward, Ashton saw that the man was heavy-set, and a long beard covered his broad face. He had large, dark eyes that were deeply set on either side of a broad nose. His clothes were made from animal hides and furs.

"Howdy," Ashton said.

The trapper stopped his horse but kept his rifle at a ready position.

"My name is John Ashton. I'm building that ranch down below."

"Jeb Rawlings," the man answered.

"I suppose you are surprised to see ranch buildings going up."

"Nope. Heard about it."

135

Not knowing where to carry the conversation with the taciturn mountain man, Ashton invited him to dinner.

"Don't mind if I do," was the reply.

The two men did not exchange conversation again until they reached the ranch. Ashton guessed his age to be between fifty and sixty, but the growth of beard and unkempt appearance were misleading. Rawlings tended to his mule and horse and then lumbered slowly up to the ranch house. He seated himself on one of the porch chairs across from Ashton and lighted a handmade pipe. Ashton offered him a whiskey which be downed in one gulp. From that indication, Ashton guessed that filling his glass would be a full-time chore, so he had a bottle placed on a table between them.

"Good whiskey. I been a long time without a drink."

"Well, have all you want."

"Obliged," Rawlings muttered as he puffed on his pipe and let the liquor drain down his throat.

"Do you hunt or prospect up in the mountains?"

"Little o' both."

After four drinks, the old hunter became more talkative.

"Bin' hunting and prospecting in the hills for more years than you been born. Hate to see people moving in, no offense meant."

"None is taken," Ashton replied.

"Just that the game is going and too many people around. Spoils them mountains. Don't like a lot of people around."

"How often do you see people?"

"Not any oftener than I have to. You the one that shot Clay Bullard?"

"Yes."

The old man nodded his head. "Saved me the trouble. Him and them outlaws hunted me more than once in the hills. Thought they'd get my gold."

Rawlings let out a low, growl of a laugh.

"All the time I was behind them. They didn't know how to track. Once I left a skunk pinned to a tree to let em' know what I thought of them. They was really mad." Rawlings downed another drink.

"You say they were trying to hunt you?"

"Yup. Thought I had a lot of gold. Ain't much gold up there. Jist enough for me to buy supplies now and then."

"Did you have any scrapes with them?"

"Shot two of them over the years. One of them died. Saw where they buried him. That Clay Bullard had it in his mind to hunt me down. Kind of a game to them until I shot 'em. Since you come on the scene, ain't had no trouble with them," Rawlings said.

Ashton saw the point of the joke and laughed.

"Even though they come after you now and then, you still intend to stay up in the mountains hunting and prospecting?"

"Yup. I was there before they came, and I'll be there after they're dead."

That evening Rawlings had dinner with Ashton and his crew and ate enough for two men. After

137

dinner, Ashton, Ben Mathews, and Jeb Rawlings sat on the veranda enjoying the cool evening air.

"There are plenty of extra beds in the bunkhouse, Jeb," Ashton offered.

"I'll sleep out in the grass. Can't sleep in a bed no more. Ain't comfortable."

"Have breakfast with us before you head into town tomorrow."

"I'll do that."

The men were silent for a few moments, each lost in his own thoughts.

"You kin' expect some trouble soon," Rawlings said.

"How's that?" Mathews asked.

"Seen a lot of activity goin' on in Bullard's camp before I left the mountains."

"You were in their hideout?" Ashton asked.

"Nope. Was above it. Wanted to see how many of them I might run into going out of the mountains."

"From what I understand, Bullard's hideout can't be reached except by riding through a narrow pass that's guarded all the time," Mathews said.

"That's right. But, you kin' climb to a point on the rim of the canyon and look down in."

"Is there a path down inside?" Ashton asked.

"Nope. Ain't no path in. But you could get in. Risky though."

"How?" Mathews asked.

"Need a couple hundred feet of rope. You could lower yourself down one ledge at a time," Rawlings said. "One false step and you'd go down in a hurry."

Ashton and Mathews looked at each other.

"It would take a desperate man to want to get in that way," Rawlings said.

"Could you show me how to get to that location if I ever needed to?" Ashton asked.

"Yup," Rawlings replied and drained his glass again.

Ashton got up and came back with a fresh bottle, thinking that if Rawlings visited often the liquor supply would suffer a major setback.

"You say a couple men could probably be lowered down into the canyon?"

"Have to be at night, or you would be seen right away. Doing it at night is what makes it so risky. Have to be sure-footed. If you fell, you'd be flat as a pancake."

Ashton was silent as he thought of the possibilities. Mathews and Ashton exchanged glances but said nothing.

"Well, reckon I'll turn in," Rawlings said.

The three men got up from their seats and said their good-nights. Ashton and Mathews then sat down again and rolled cigarettes.

"Say what's on your mind, Ben."

Mathews turned in his chair and stared intently at Ashton in the half-light coming through the window.

"Let's go with Rawlings and locate the area where we can get down in the canyon. The information could be vital, and if they're hunting the old man like he says, they just might get him one of these days. Then the information would be lost."

"I doubt that they will catch him. He's too

shrewd."

"Then, suppose the old man just dies of natural causes?"

"He's too mean to die."

Jess Bullard rode at the head of the long column of men as they wound slowly through the stands of aspen and pine trees making their way down from the high country. The pace was slow, and the men often stopped as Bullard would study the rough timber country for signs of other riders. There was little conversation during the day-long ride. The men were engrossed in their own thoughts. The majority of them had not wanted to attack the Ashton ranch for fear of the obviously strong opposition and probable retaliation. Nevertheless, Bullard led through brute force.

"Anyone not saddled and ready to ride in half an hour will deal with me," he had told the assembled outlaws. All had been ready except for the men wanted in other states, who were not part of Bullard's outlaw band.

Now, the column headed south through the mountains, and the timber began to thin as they descended to a lower elevation. They came to a creek and followed as it widened into a pool surrounded by multi-colored rock formations. The timber was sparse, and the small hills were boulder-strewn. Bullard dismounted, and the other riders followed. He posted guards upstream and down and then climbed a rock formation and studied the country to the east. As the afternoon grew longer and the sun began to set, the mountains cast long shadows eastward.

As dusk neared, Bullard again climbed the large rock and could see a small group of riders crossing the range country coming toward him. The group of riders traveled single file as they followed a narrow trail through the rocky country and finally arrived at the water hole. In the lead was Jeff Starbuck. The eight Starbuck riders dismounted and watered their horses. Bullard and Starbuck exchanged greetings and walked to one side to talk.

"I expected you'd have more men," said Bullard. "Your father must have four times this many riders."

"There were problems."

Bullard said nothing, waiting for the young man to explain.

"My father fired Ford Gentry."

"What?" Bullard asked in his gruff voice.

"Dad wanted him to lead the men, and he refused. When my father told the cowboys what he was planning to do, not many of them were anxious to buck Ashton. He couldn't fire the ones who refused to go, because someone might warn Ashton. So, this is all the men I have."

"Well, we should have enough. Twenty-four men is more than twice the number Ashton has on his ranch. We'll ride in about four in the morning and set fire to the ranch house and the other buildings. It should be easy to pick them off in the fire light."

Starbuck nodded his agreement.

"Did he agree to the split?" Bullard asked as his

eyes bore into the young man.

"Yes. You and your men will get two-thirds of Ashton's cattle. We will keep the rest."

It was nearly midnight before Jeb Rawlings arrived back at the Ashton ranch. He had followed Bullard's men throughout the day. His mountain experience allowed him to stay close to the outlaws without being detected, and he had been almost near enough to hear the conversation between Bullard and Starbuck when the two groups met. From the hand motions the men used as they talked, he was sure they meant to attack Ashton's ranch. He was now in Ashton's ranch house. Ben Mathews and Jamie McDonald had joined the two men.

"How many are there?" Ashton asked.

"Two dozen. I counted. Only a third of 'em are Starbuck riders."

Ashton's face was lined, and he was tired, as were the other men, from branding calves for the past few days. But his eyes were hard and his mouth was drawn to a fine line.

"It's strange that there are so few Starbuck riders," Mathews replied.

"Not so," the old man answered. "Ain't many of 'em want to tangle with you. You're developin' a reputation."

"You think the attack will be this evening?" Ashton asked.

"Sure of it. They met and were gettin' ready to sleep early. That means they'll be gettin' up early," said Rawlings.

"My guess is the attack will be about three or four in the morning," Ashton speculated.

Rawlings nodded in agreement.

"They had a number of jugs of coal oil with 'em. Figure they mean to burn you out."

Ashton stood with his hands on his hips contemplating what defensive plan to institute. The other men sat quietly watching him. Ashton turned around and looked at Rawlings.

"I want to thank you for bringing us this information. I realize you took a great risk and deeply appreciate it. But this is not your fight, and you certainly are not expected to participate. There is no reason why you should take any more risks."

Rawlings grinned.

"Reckon I'll stay if you don't mind. Haven't been in a good fight in sometime."

Ashton smiled and said, "We'll be glad to have you."

McDonald spoke for the first time.

"If there are twelve of us and twenty-four of them, the numbers should be about equal."

Ashton grinned and looked at Mathews.

"Ben, get the men and bring them here along with all the arms and ammunition. We'll discuss a little strategy."

12

Bullard was at the front of the column of men as they quietly dismounted near the rear of the barn. A full moon outlined the ranch buildings which cast black shadows. Two of the night riders moved slowly towards the bunkhouse. Bullard then motioned several other men to go to the ranch house, and they complied. The men's shadows drifted away and blended in with other obscure images. The night was quiet except for the chirping crickets and other insects.

Less than a minute elapsed before one of Bullard's men came on the run back to the barn.

He reached the giant, bear-like man and blurted out, "Somethin' funny going on. Nobody in the bunkhouse . . ."

Before he finished the sentence, a volley of gunfire exploded from the ranch house, and a long, piercing scream indicated that the bullets had found their mark.

Bullard was behind the barn and reacted quickly to surprise.

"Clint. Get back over there and fire up that bunkhouse. Starbuck, you take your men and get around behind the ranch house. Try to move in close enough to set fire to it. My men will move in

144

from the two sides."

"Let's go," Starbuck yelled to his men. They began running in a long circle to get in position.

Bullard's men began returning the fire from the house. The evening was filled with bright flashes of flame, and the gunfire grew to a roar. Suddenly, the bunkhouse burst into flame, and the fire lighted the yard with wavering streaks of light.

"Breed, take five men and get around to the left side of the house. Brandt, you and Williams stay here. The rest of you come with me," Bullard ordered.

Just outside of the ring of light, the outlaws ran to take their positions.

The fire blazed higher, and the night's blackness was stripped away. Two bodies were visible in front of the ranch house, one lying partially on the front porch with his head and arms in the dirt at the base of the steps. The first round of firing had taken the men at point blank range and hurled them back.

New firing erupted from the rear of the house as Starbuck and his men got in position. Starbuck rolled on his side and spoke to the man next to him.

"Light that lantern, and run up a ways and throw it at the ranch house. We'll cover you with heavy fire into the windows."

The man was breathing hard as he looked at Starbuck with fear.

"Move!" Starbuck shouted.

The cowboy crawled to his knees, lit the lantern, and ran forward a few yards to throw it. He extended his arm behind him preparatory to throwing the missile just as gunfire erupted from both rear windows. The slugs threw him backward, and he landed on top of the lantern. In seconds, the dead man's clothes were ablaze, and Starbuck's riders crawled backward away from the fire.

Inside the cabin, Ben Mathews was directing the operations from a defensive standpoint. In a crouched position, he went from room to room checking the men. The side opposite Bullard and his main group of gunmen began coming under stronger fire, and Mathews guessed they would try to fire up the cabin from that side, which had only one window. Mathews brought Brad Prince and Randy Miller from the front living room into the side bedroom. The firing became more intense, and slugs made shrill humming sounds as they zinged through the open window and buried themselves in the opposite wall. The room was becoming clouded with smoke from the rapid firing, and the blasting of the guns made hearing almost impossible.

Ted Marston, one of Ashton's cavalry riders, suddenly fell backwards clutching his face. Mathews rushed over to him and in the dim light could see he was dead.

Outside in the blackness Ashton, together with Jamie McDonald, Jeb Rawlings, and Bill Autry, had crawled up behind Bullard and his main group. The four men had waited, lying in the high grass, until they could determine exactly where the most assistance was needed. They had moved around behind Bullard's main assemblage when it appeared this would be the weakest defensive position.

"Don't fire until they light the lanterns and get ready to throw them," he told his men.

Several matches were struck, and three lanterns spread their light among the outlaw group.

"Now," Bullard yelled at his men.

The outlaws threw the missiles just as Ashton and his men fired a volley. Two of the men yelled, and all three went down. Bullard's force was now in a state of confusion. Ashton and his men continued to rain rifle shots into the outlaw group, and the outlaws began to crawl off in different directions while attempting to return the fire.

"That's enough," Ashton shouted, and he and his men again retreated into the darkness.

They ran in a long half-circle until they came up behind Breed Saterlee and his men. Saterlee's group had been methodically firing at the ranch house but had made no move to go forward. Again, Ashton and his three men sent a hail of gunfire into the outlaw band, and they broke and ran. The firing now had died down as more than half the outlaws attempted to find refuge out of range of gunfire.

Jeff Starbuck was confused and fearful that other riders had joined the fight.

"Circle around to the horses," Starbuck instructed his men. "We're getting out of here."

Starbuck's men rose from the grass and began running to their horses. Ashton's group poured gunfire after them, and there was increased firing from the house as the barricaded men realized that the tide of battle had turned. The outlaws converged on the barn, and the men were swearing, and some were moaning because of their wounds.

Jeff Starbuck could make out Bullard's huge figure in the now dim firelight.

"What the hell happened?"

"Don't ask stupid questions," the outlaw leader bellowed as he mounted his horse. "Tell your father his idea stank."

Men now emerged from the ranch house and joined with Ashton in firing at the retreating outlaws.

Suddenly the shooting stopped, and the quiet was almost worse than repeated gunfire.

Mathews looked at Ashton, and his eyes gleamed from a face streaked with sweat and grime.

"We did it," Mathews said.

Ashton smiled but said nothing. His chest continued to heave from the exertion of running.

"What's the situation like inside?" Ashton asked.

"Ted Marston is dead, and Bill Demory and Jack Preston are wounded, but not real bad," Mathews replied. "The bunkhouse is burned down, and there are a lot of holes in the ranch house. But I would say we did real good."

Ashton nodded his head in agreement.

The wounded men were administered to, and Doctor Henderson was sent for. Ashton and Jeb Rawlings searched the area around the ranch house and counted seven bodies. An eighth outlaw was found alive but badly wounded and died before morning.

At daybreak, the men were still cleaning up the ranch area. A large trench was dug a quarter mile from the ranch, and the outlaws were buried in a common grave. Another grave nearer the ranch house was dug for Ted Marston. They had defeated a much larger force of men and won the decisive battle necessary for the continued existence of the ranch.

Ashton poured himself a cup of steaming coffee. Jeb Rawlings approached him holding a bottle in one hand and a tin cup in the other.

"You sure serve good liquor," Rawlings said. His eyes twinkled.

The two men faced each other, and a feeling of understanding and mutual admiration passed between them.

"Thanks," Ashton said.

"Best fight I bin' in in a long time. What are you planning to do now?"

Ashton's eyes narrowed as he gazed at the mountains.

"I guess it's time for you to show me Bullard's hideout."

Jeff Starbuck led his four remaining riders into the ranch yard and dismounted. He was tired and angry at the defeat. His hatred for Ashton had grown to a magnitude where it now rivaled his father's. As he walked up the steps of the ranch house, he was not looking forward to the confrontation with his father. Yet the battle seemed to have matured him. He was beginning to feel the power of authority, and a sense of responsibility was growing in him. He realized that the senseless range war with Ashton could not be won.

Ezra Starbuck sat slumped behind his desk. Jeff was shocked by his father's appearance. The cattle baron seemed to have aged ten years in the past forty-eight hours. His eyes appeared sunken, and large dark rings were prominent under the eyes. His face was lined and he looked exhausted. Jeff stared at his father for a few moments before he spoke.

"We got beat."

"I could tell that by looking at the group of you when you rode in. What happened?"

"They were waiting for us. I don't know how they knew we were coming, but they did. The bunch of them were in the ranch house. We surrounded it, and I think we could have burned it down. But, some other riders came up and joined the fight. We were caught in a cross fire and . . ."

"And ran!" Ezra Starbuck shouted.

The old man pulled himself up from the chair and leaned on the desk.

"Three of my men got shot down, and you ran," he yelled.

"No. We didn't lose three men in the fight, only one. The other two decided they didn't want to work for Starbuck Ranch any longer and rode on," Jeff said in a loud voice.

"No man quits this ranch without my permission."

"Well, get used to the fact that two of them just did."

"Who are they?"

Jeff took a deep breath and exhaled sharply.

"Does it really matter, father?"

"I want answers," Starbuck yelled.

"This fight isn't getting us anywhere. You've lost face, Ford Gentry is gone and the ranch is starting to fall apart piece by piece. Try to use some good judgment for a change."

Ezra Starbuck was speechless. His son had never spoken to him like that before, and in his irrational state, something snapped in his mind. He grabbed a whip off the wall behind him and began staggering towards Jeff.

"I'll teach you to talk to me that way."

Jeff took a step backwards, and his heel caught in the edge of a large rug in the center of the room.

"Put that whip down. You've laid a hand on me for the last time."

The old man shook the coils out of the whip and kept advancing. Jeff Starbuck drew his revolver and cocked it.

"You've bullied me for the last time. Stay where you are."

Starbuck stopped momentarily, not believing that his son would draw a gun on him.

"You're worthless, and you haven't got the guts to pull the trigger."

Starbuck lashed out with the whip, and Jeff jerked backwards. But his foot caught in the heavy fringe on the rug, and his muscles contracted as he attempted to keep himself from falling. His revolver fired and the blast filled the room with smoke. The bullet hit Ezra Starbuck in the chest. The ranch owner raised his arms, his eyes bulged

151

out and his mouth was wide open from the shock. A loud growl came from his mouth as he fell forward on his face.

Momentarily, Jeff was frozen to the spot where he stood. Then he dropped his gun and rushed to his father. He carefully rolled the old man over to his back.

"It was an accident. I'm sorry."

Ezra Starbuck's lifeless eyes stared at the ceiling.

Jeff held the old man in his arms and began crying.

"Why didn't you love me? Why? I tried. I really did. It's just that nothing turned out right," Jeff Starbuck's voice was choked with tears.

Caroline Starbuck, followed by the cook, burst into the office.

"Father!" she cried.

Ford Gentry finished giving instructions to the cowhands and sent them on their way. It had been two days since Caroline Starbuck's message had reached him, and the next forty-eight hours had allowed him little time for sleep. He was now the unquestioned leader at the ranch, and all decisions fell to him. Gentry had made arrangements for the funeral, which was to be held the following day and sent out one rider after another to nearby ranches, informing the ranchers of the time and place.

Sheriff Jim Mayberry had visited the ranch the night of the killing and came back again the following day after Gentry had returned and assumed command. Mayberry had been unable to find Jeff Starbuck.

"Got any idea where he might be?" Mayberry had asked.

Gentry's mouth had tightened into a sharp line and he said, "No."

"You knew them better than anyone else. Do you think it was an accident?"

"Ezra wasn't himself towards the end. It's possible that he went at Jeff with a whip. There was one laying near the body, Caroline said. Jeff might have accidentally pulled the trigger."

"When I find him, there will have to be a coroner's inquest to determine the facts of the case. There will probably be no charges filed against Jeff if it happened like he said."

Ford Gentry was thinking about the conversation now as more riders arrived at the ranch. He swore softly to himself. Why don't they leave her alone until the funeral, he thought. It's hard enough on her as it is. This is no time for visits.

He made the visitors comfortable in the house, and they were met by Caroline's aunt, Maybell Carter, who had made the trip from the adjoining county to be with Caroline.

Gentry excused himself and walked over to the bunkhouse. He sent two riders to the south range to check on the cattle in that section and dispatched another to town for additional supplies.

The range war was over, he thought to himself as he walked back to the ranch house. It had ended poorly for Starbuck Ranch, but he intended to pull things back together and get the spread running smoothly again in time. What will happen to Jeff? The question kept running through his mind. He felt sorry for the boy, for the recent events had not been of his making. Swept up in a tide of hatred, Jeff had been the target of his father's frustrations and broken pride. The despair he is feeling now must be a terrible thing, Gentry thought.

A Starbuck rider entered the yard at a gallop. Gentry walked out to meet him. The rider dismounted.

"He's waiting for you over the hill," the cowhand said and pointed to the location.

"Nobody is to know about this, Dan," Gentry said quietly as he studied the cowboy. That's why I picked you for this assignment. You know when to keep your mouth shut and have always been a loyal Starbuck rider. I need loyal men right now."

"I understand," the cowboy replied.

Gentry mounted his horse and left instructions that he would return in a few minutes. About a quarter of a mile from the ranch he rode up a small hill and saw a lone rider awaiting him at the bottom. Gentry rode over to him and dismounted. Ford Gentry and John Ashton looked at each other momentarily and said nothing.

"I appreciate your coming. I know this is rather unusual under the circumstances," Gentry said. "I couldn't leave the ranch, but I had to talk to you."

"I understand, Ford. I know you have all types of problems on your hands at the moment."

Gentry got out the makings for a cigarette and offered his tobacco to Ashton. The two men rolled cigarettes.

"First of all, I wasn't involved in any of the things that happened to you or at your ranch."

"I believe you."

"My rider explained to you what occurred. Ezra is dead, and Jeff is gone."

Ashton nodded his head and exhaled smoke.

"Caroline is head of the ranch now, and I'll run it for her. You will have no more trouble from Starbuck Ranch."

"I understand what you are saying, Ford. Now, you want to know where I stand."

"That's right."

Ashton was quiet for a moment while he gathered his thoughts. Then he looked at Gentry.

"One of my cowhands was killed during that raid, and two others were wounded. I intend to see that the men who planned and carried out that raid are brought to justice. I owe that much to my men even if we do call a truce."

Gentry flipped his cigarette away. The smoke burned his dry throat.

"You deserve to know the full story. Jeff led seven men from our ranch on the raid. One was killed and two others headed out after the fight. Jeff brought the other four back, and then the incident occurred when Ezra was killed. The next morning when I found out what happened, I fired those four and sent them packing. There are no longer any men on Starbuck Ranch that participated in the raid."

Ashton said nothing as he looked out over the grasslands.

155

"Seems crazy that men should fight and die over this land when there is so much of it, Ford."

"Yup," Gentry answered. "But some people have to try to be king of the hill."

"Well, it's about over. As far as I'm concerned the Ashton Ranch and the Starbuck Ranch can live side by side without fighting."

"I took my job back under those conditions," Gentry replied.

"Then it's settled," Ashton said, holding out his hand.

The two men shook hands and smiled.

13

The funeral was well attended by nearly one hundred ranchers, townspeople, relatives and cowboys arrayed in their finest attire. They listened to the Rev. Andrew McIntosh deliver a lengthy eulogy full of high praises and acclaim for the accomplishments, laudable character, and abundant services performed by Ezra Starbuck. Women cried softly, and men nodded their heads in approval and agreement as the clergyman droned on and on.

Caroline Starbuck stood erect and untouchable at the center of a small group of immediate relatives. Throughout the mornning she had moved smoothly among the guests as they arrived. Her countenance was flawless. She appeared in total command of her emotions, and many of those who attended had marveled at her apparent strength and bearing. She was the true daughter of Ezra Starbuck.

Ann Winter stood beside her father as the service neared the halfway point. In the sweltering heat, she and the other women were feeling the choking effects of the black veils and most had raised them. She felt Caroline's gaze upon her and slowly moved her eyes to the other woman.

Caroline's unfeeling eyes now were fixed upon Ann. Ann returned the look, wondering what agony Caroline must be experiencing. But Caroline's stare was unwavering, and after nearly a minute, Ann realized that she was the recipient of a message that she did not entirely understand. Ann returned her attention to the service, but soon sensed that she was being watched. She again looked at Caroline, and her perception was more acute.

She hates me, Ann thought. What would prompt her to think in that way? Ann knew that Caroline Starbuck had always hated to lose. She had lost her father and brother and . . . John Ashton! She thinks I've won and she has lost, Ann thought. Ann deliberately shifted her attention away from Caroline. I don't wish to continue this, Ann thought.

After what seemed to be an eternity, the eulogy ended, and the funeral ceremonies came to an end with the burying of Ezra Starbuck in the family plot. The women then adjourned to the house, while the men headed for the stable and whiskey that was provided under Ford Gentry's orders. The conversation was subdued and centered around the weather, cattle, and the coming election. Everything was touched upon by the men except the subject on their minds—the Starbuck Ranch and its owners. Ford Gentry made the rounds of the groups, listening to the men wish him well and express their sorrow at the passing of Ezra Starbuck.

Because of the distance between ranches,

towns, and settlements, funerals and weddings were top social events when friends who had not seen each other for long periods could get together. At noon the mourners passed through long lines for food and drink and sat at large, hastily assembled tables. In the early afternoon the first of the families began to leave to make the long trips back to to their homes.

Ann Winter and her father were among the first to pay their parting respects to Caroline Starbuck and her immediate relatives. The exchange of conversation between Ann and Caroline was brief and perfunctory, and Ann was glad the ordeal had come to a conclusion. She climbed into the buggy, her father joined her, and they set off along the trail leading back to town.

On the hill overlooking the trail as it wound away from the ranch, two men sat on their horses watching the people depart from the funeral. Jake Miles, and a second rider, Lou Edwards, looked at one another as the Winter buggy moved along the trail below them.

"I don't know why Bullard wants us to grab that girl," Miles said nervously. His eyes continued to dart anxiously from side to side.

"I can guess," Edwards said slowly. He was an ordinary-looking cowboy of medium height and build. He had shoulder length brown hair and a brown moustache that almost covered his bottom lip. One characteristic set him aside from the ordinary cowhand. His deeply set dark eyes settled firmly on an object and never wavered. The natural contempt and dislike for ordinary people was evident in his eyes; men were immediately fearful of him.

"Where do you want to do it?" Miles asked.

"Between the next set of hills," Edwards answered. "Is this girl pretty?"

"Yeah. But you know what Bullard said. Nothing is to happen to her. We are to leave the message with her father and see that she comes with us to the Owlhoots," Miles said.

"Been a long time since I had a woman," Edwards said as he turned his head to look at Miles.

Looking into the hard eyes, Miles suddenly dropped his gaze.

"You know what the boss said," Miles answered.

"I don't think he ever means to return that woman. It'll make no difference," said Edwards.

"Get it out of your mind, Lou. Bullard has killed men for not carrying out his orders."

"His days are numbered. You can smell it. This country is about to come down on him, and his days as top dog are about done."

"Don't kid yourself, Lou."

"Let's ride," Edwards said.

For the next forty-five minutes, the two outlaws circled through the low hills and arrived at a point next to a small stand of trees. They waited silently until the noise of the buggy wheels on the rocks was almost upon them and then rode out and blocked the trail.

Thurman Winter quickly reigned in the horse and stopped his buggy. He was visibly frightened but remained silent. Miles rode up to the buggy and lifted Winter's rifle from the interior.

"Old man, get down from that buggy," Edwards ordered.

"See here! What do you men want? I have very little money with me."

Ann had said nothing to this point, but had recognized Miles.

"Get down," Edwards repeated.

"Do as they say father."

"I'll do nothing of the kind. You men leave us alone," Winter said in a frightened voice. He was wide-eyed, and sweat stood out on his forehead.

Miles stepped down from his horse and walked slowly up to the buggy. His eyes never left Ann Winter, and she glared back at him with disgust.

"You'd best do as you're told."

Edwards walked his horse over to the buggy and suddenly reached out and grabbed Thurman Winter by the arm. He pulled hard, and the slender man pitched out of the buggy and landed in the dust on his hands and knees. At the same instant, Ann grabbed the buggy whip and slashed Miles across the face. The outlaw let out a scream of rage and whirled around. Although half blinded, his peripheral vision saw the horse and rider approaching from the front. Through tearing eyes, Miles recognized the rider.

"Don't shoot, Edwards. I know him," Miles warned.

Jeff Starbuck rode forward at a slow pace and stopped about twenty feet in front of the buggy. Shocked as Ann Winter was over the previous occurrence, she was still stunned over Starbuck's

161

appearance. His blond hair was stringy and matted and poked out from under his hat at various angles. Jeff's clothing was torn and filthy from being slept in on the range for the past days. Starbuck's face was gaunt and haggard. His cheek bones protruded from the emaciated face. Jeff's lips were drawn tightly together until his mouth was almost a slit. Looking into his sad, dejected eyes, Ann felt a deep sorrow.

The entire scene had come to a halt as Starbuck rode up. Even Thurman Winter made no motion to rise from the dirt. He stared up at Jeff, not believing how grotesque the young man had become.

A change suddenly came over Jeff's features as he looked away from Ann and viewed the two outlaws. Edwards perceived what was happening and his right hand moved slowly towards his holster.

"Get away from there, Miles," Starbuck ordered.

"You don't understand, Jeff. Bullard ordered us to get the girl and take her back to the Owlhoots. We're here under his orders."

"No," Starbuck said in a hoarse whisper.

"Jeff, back off and stay out of this," Miles warned.

Starbuck shifted his attention back to Ann. His penetrating stare contained a longing and at the same time a helplessness. He was a drowning man being pulled under, and he recognized the hopelessness of his situation. Jeff's eyes told her of his love in the brief instant.

In a moment the spell was broken. His attention

went back to the two outlaws, and a wild, almost crazy glint showed in his eyes. Jeff's face became twisted in his anger.

Still not wanting to fight openly unless all else failed, Jake Miles raised his hands, palms outward, and motioned for Starbuck to back off.

"Jeff, wait a minute," Miles pleaded.

Edwards, realizing that Starbuck would make a fight of it, made his decision and acted. In one fluid motion, his revolver appeared in his hand, and the gun's blast set the scene into a whirl of motion. But Starbuck had not been taken by surprise. He had sighted Edwards' drawing motion, and his own reflex was instantaneous. His revolver fired in return a split second later.

The bullet from Edwards' revolver struck Jeff in the left shoulder and almost pitched him off the horse backwards. His slug struck Edwards in the stomach, and the outlaw let out a sharp cry as he grabbed the saddle horn. Edward's horse started running, and the outlaw dropped his gun as he tried to keep from being pitched into the dirt.

"Damm you, Jeff!" Miles yelled, reaching for his revolver.

The horse pulling the buggy reared with fright at the first short, and Starbuck was having difficulty staying on his horse. The whirl of activity encompassed them all, including Thurman Winter who had gotten back on his feet and scrambled towards the buggy.

Miles entered the combat for the first time. His first shot missed Starbuck, but the second bullet went through Jeff's chest. As Starbuck was falling from his horse he fired one last shot, and the slug smashed into Miles' forehead. The outlaw was propelled backward and landed on his back in the dust.

"Jeff!" Ann yelled in an anguished voice.

She jumped from the buggy and ran to him. Ann gently took his head and shoulders in her arms. Tears were streaming down her cheeks. A smile broke across Jeff's dirt-smeared face.

"You do care," he whispered.

"Yes," she said softly and nodded her head.

"It's better this way," he said, coughing. "I couldn't go on, the way things were. Want you to know something. It was an accident. Didn't mean to . . ."

Starbuck's voice trailed off into a raspy cough.

"I believe you, Jeff."

He smiled again and slowly reached up and touched her cheek with his fingers. Then his hand went limp and he was gone. Ann cried softly and held him tightly.

Two riders came around a bend in the trail, their horses traveling at top speed. Thurman Winter ran to meet them.

John Ashton walked swiftly through the store and into the rear living quarters.

"Ann," he said as she rushed into his arms.

They held each other tightly.

"Thank God, you're alright."

"Don't stop holding me," she said.

Ashton stroked her hair. After a few moments she pulled her head back and looked into his eyes.

"He was very brave at the end."

Ashton nodded his head in agreement. She rested her head against his chest.

"He told me the shooting was an accident. I believe him."

"It's my fault that this happened," he said in a firm voice.

Ann said nothing, but held him tighter.

"When will it end," she said quietly, breaking the momentary silence.

"Very soon."

She looked into his eyes and saw the hardness. Was the country changing him or had the war done so earlier?

"Let's take a ride before dark. I want to feel the openness," Ann said.

He nodded his head in agreement.

For the next two hours they rode through the grasslands, stopping now and then to walk the horses. She spoke of her life in the community, her hopes, expectations, likes and dislikes, and about her father. They stopped to water the horses, and Ann sat with her back against a giant cottonwood tree. He sensed that she was trying to tell him something, but he was unable to penetrate her mind. Ashton waited patiently, knowing she was about ready to get to the point.

Suddenly, she stopped talking, leaned her head back against the tree. Her eyes filled with tears.

"I'm leaving," she said softly.

Ashton stiffened, but remained standing in the same spot.

"The danger is past for you, Ann. There won't be another try, and we are about ready to move against Bullard. The danger isn't there anymore."

"It's not just that. I'm tired of the killing, of the way this country has changed. Death follows you, John."

Ashton gritted his teeth and felt his stomach churn.

"A man has to make his way. I came here peacefully. I intend to stay."

He was single-minded and his firm convictions governed his actions. Subtle differences and distinctions did not bother him.

The sky was beginning to turn orange as the last afternoon changed to the early stages of twilight. Ann's face reflected the coming event as soft shadows brushed her features. It was out now, and she knew she had to continue, to explain, to make him understand.

"The country has changed," she repeated. "The people aren't the same. Neighbors are suspicious of one another. The atmosphere is unhealthy. I don't want to be a part of this unhappiness any longer. I'm leaving for St. Louis in two days to live with my aunt. Right now, I just want to get away."

Ashton lowered himself to one knee and rested his arm on it. He felt at a loss to know what to tell her. His self-assurance was shaken.

"I don't want you to go."

Ann looked at him with a pained expression.

"I don't want to go, either. But I am. When I'm with you, I feel wonderful. When we are apart, I'm worried like I have never worried before. It isn't right."

The early evening breezes began to rise and made her hair dance around the edges of her face. It made her all the more desirable to him, and he wanted desperately to reach out and touch her, to take her in his arms and feel the quickening response. But his pride held him back. At this moment, Ashton was a prisoner of his own strengths, his self-reliance, and his unyielding belief that he was right. She sensed what he was thinking.

"You're shutting me out," she said softly.

"What do you expect of me?"

"I suppose I expected more. I thought you were someone you aren't. I believed that you were sensitive, fair, and understanding," she said as her voice began to waver. "But you kill, and you keep on killing."

Ashton took one step forward, grabbed her, and pulled her close to him. She was sobbing quietly, her head on his chest.

"You've been through too much. It's my fault. But try not to judge me too harshly. This is rough country, and a man has to either meet the challenge or crumble. Your father is a good example."

The last sentence slipped out before he had a chance to stop it. It was an honest statement on his part, not meant to hurt her or malign her father. The example had just flashed into his mind. But he felt her stiffen, and as she looked at him the anger was noticeable in her eyes. She pushed away from him.

"Leave my father out of this. He had nothing to do with my decision. My father is a good, decent man, a civilized person who has never harmed another individual in his life," she said in an even voice.

"I'm sorry. I didn't mean it the way it sounded."

A short time later, they mounted their horses and rode back to town. It was a quiet trip. For the most part, each was lost in his and her own thoughts. As they stopped in front of Thurman Winter's store, Ben Mathews stepped through the door and faced Ashton. He was heavily armed, and from the look on his face Ashton knew something was wrong.

Ashton helped Ann Winter dismount, and for a moment they looked at one another. She appeared resolute, yet the pain was there. The moment ended, and with great reluctance she turned and walked into the store. Mathews walked quickly up to Ashton.

"Bullard's men killed Jamie McDonald."

14

Jess Bullard led six men along a winding trail about half way up the Owlhoots. Returning from a profitable trade of stolen cattle for cash to the west of Desert City, the outlaw leader had not yet learned of the bungled kidnap attempt. The men rested their horses, smoked, and viewed the foothills below them. The huge outlaw leader detected movement on a trail hundreds of feet below, and minutes later was able to follow the progress of two riders, apparently headed in the direction he had just come from. He pondered the situation for a moment and then looked around at his men. By now, they had also noticed the riders.

"Stark. Ride back along our trail until you get close enough to get a look. You been in town a lot. If it's Ashton or any of his men, signal with this mirror, and we'll meet you where the trails cross," Bullard ordered.

The reluctant outlaw mounted and rode back down the trail. His descending route continued at an angle for more than two miles before it joined the foothills trail. An hour and a half later he was situated in a stand of pines near the junction of the two trails as Ashton's men, Jamie McDonald, and Brad Prince came into view. Stark studied the men carefully and recognized them. He waited until they had passed out of sight among the trees, then rode out into an open spot and flashed the sun's rays back up the mountain to the spot where Bullard waited.

Receiving the signal, Bullard ordered his men into the saddle. They traveled up along the rising trail until it reached the summit and then started downgrade. Bullard's route took him over the mountain and down the other side. They maintained their rapid pace in hopes of cutting off the two men before they rode out of the foothills and on to the flats.

The horses were about played out by the time Bullard and his men reached the spot the outlaw leader had in mind. They dismounted in a ravine, climbed to the hilltop, and looked down at the trail one hundred and fifty yards below them. Behind the outlaws, the mountain rose sharply. They waited nearly fifteen minutes before the two men came into view. McDonald and Prince rode slowly, talking and laughing as the trail proceeded out of the foothills. On their way to Desert City for supplies, the partners had scorned the safe road that circled the mountain range and decided to travel the foothills route that was only half as long. Young, flushed with success at their victory, and confident of their abilities, they had disregarded Ashton's warning about traveling only trails on the flats.

McDonald was in the lead. He took off his hat and wiped his forehead. Prince was the more alert of the two, constantly checking the surrounding small hills and his own back trail.

Bullard's eyes narrowed as he watched the two cowboys coming closer. Like a wild animal, his senses were alert, and he was bent on killing.

"Don't anybody shoot until I give the word," he growled in a low voice.

Two minutes later the cowboys were directly below the outlaws.

"I'm thinking of a cold beer, a real cold beer," McDonald said as he looked back at Prince and smiled.

The blast from Bullard's rifle was immediately followed by a volley from the other outlaws. Bullard's shot struck McDonald in the lower chest area, pitching him off his horse. Another slug killed the animal immediately, and the big gelding went down and off the side of the trail. McDonald was able to crawl behind the animal and pull out his Winchester rifle.

Prince bad been luckier. As the first rifle cracked, he pulled his Winchester out and threw himself out of the saddle. One slug whistled by his head, and another smashed into his right leg as he came off the horse. He rolled into a gully formed by the water's runoff from the mountains. His horse also was hit and went down screaming and thrashing on the trail.

"Jamie! How bad are you hit?" Prince yelled.

"I'll be alright. Watch out for yourself," McDonald answered.

Bullard's crew continued to fire. Some of the bullets whacked into McDonald's dead horse, sounding like blows being landed in a fist fight.

171

Others ricocheted off the rocky ground, sending the projectiles hurling in different directions. Each ricochet had a separate, distinctive sound.

McDonald was bleeding heavily, and his efforts to stop the flow of blood were unsuccessful. Surprisingly the big redhead was not in a great deal of pain. He twisted around until he was lying on his left side, levered a shell into the chamber, and raised his head enough to see the top of the hill where the outlaws were firing from. They're lousy shots. Have I got a surprise for them, he thought.

Not a shot had been returned, and Bullard's men, thinking their opponents were incapable of resistance, had gotten to their feet or were kneeling as they continued to fire. Suddenly, a rifle with a redhead behind it appeared over the back of the dead horse. McDonald fired quickly and disappeared behind the horse. His slug struck an outlaw, Ike Harris, in the heart and pitched him over backwards. Harris was dead before he hit the ground. The stunned outlaws dove for cover.

"Pick your shots and stay down," Bullard growled.

Prince used his bandanna to stop the bleeding from his leg and then began to return the outlaws' fire. His shots zinged over the crest of the hill or plowed into the hilltop, sending showers of dirt over the outlaws.

"Are you still alright, Jamie?" Prince yelled.

"Yeah," came the reply.

Twice McDonald rolled up to a position where he could fire at the hilltop, and his second shot knocked one of the outlaw's hats off. But he was losing strength rapidly and double vision was beginning to afflict him. McDonald attempted to roll into position for a third shot, but his legs would not move. He pushed the rifle over the horse and fired blindly at the top of the hill. His strength was about gone now, and he had difficulty working the lever-action of the Winchester.

"Keep firing, Brad," McDonald yelled.

Oscar Stark, the outlaw who had scouted McDonald and Prince, had stayed comfortably behind them as he followed. When the shooting began, he rode close enough to view the standoff and then circled and came up behind the two cowboys. Seeing that McDonald was not moving, Stark crept closer to the edge of the gully from which Prince would momentarily raise up, fire, and drop back. Stark slowly stood up and aimed his revolver but never fired. A bullet smashed into his stomach, and Stark was pitched backward like a rag doll. He screamed once before he died. Bullard and his men switched their positions to gain a view behind them. The second boom from Jeb Rawling's buffalo gun set the outlaws in motion as one of their horses went down in a heap.

Rawlings had been above Bullard's group when they sighted the two riders and changed course to head them off. Out of curiosity, he followed the outlaws but stayed at a higher altitude out of sight. As Bullard's group prepared the ambush, he moved slowly down the mountain on his mule following one ravine and then another. About four hundred yards above the shooting scene, he pulled in behind a stand of pine trees and balanced the huge, buffalo gun over one of the large tree branches. His third shot boomed across the mountain side and was aimed at two of the outlaws who were fighting over the same horse. The bullet smashed the right shoulder of an outlaw named Jim Akers and sent him sprawling on the ground.

"Help me, Bullard!" he pleaded as he pulled himself to a sitting position.

The outlaws were caught up in a frenzy of activity as they attempted to mount the nervous horses. Bullard momentarily looked down at the fallen man, but his eyes showed no pity. The outlaw leader was in the saddle now. He yanked the reigns around and turned the horse in the direction of a nearby gully.

"Don't leave me, Bullard!" he screamed.

The other three outlaws were already racing for the gully, and Bullard was preparing to spur his horse forward when Akers yelled again:

"If you leave me, I'll tell them all I know.'

In one fluid motion, Bullard drew his revolver, aimed, and fired. The slug entered Akers' forehead with a splat and knocked him flat on his back. Bullard then spurred his horse foward and disappeared into the ravine. From far up on the hillside, Rawlings' gun boomed one last time after the retreating outlaws.

Brad Prince was confused. He knew the firing had stopped except for the loud booming of a different weapon. After he heard the outlaws ride away, he was even more confused.

"Jamie!" he called.

There was no answer.

"Can you hear me?"

When no reply came, he carefully looked over the edge of the gully, surveyed the surrounding area, and began crawling over to McDonald. The redhead was lying on his left side, his arms cradling the rifle.

"Jamie, I'm coming."

When he reached McDonald, Prince raised himself to a kneeling position and gently rolled the redhead over on his back. From the gaping chest wound, it was obvious that McDonald had bled to death. The tears streamed down Prince's face as he shook his head from side to side. A few minutes later, Rawlings found the men still in the same position.

Jamie McDonald was buried in a simple ceremony near the ranch house. The former cavalrymen sang "Rock Of Ages," and John Ashton's mind flashed back to a previous time near the end of the war, when General Jeb Stuart had been mortally wounded near Yellow Tavern. They had sung "Rock Of Ages" for Stuart, too.

He bowed his head as he listened to the Reverend say the final words. Ashton's eyelids crept closer together, and his lips tightened, giving his face a fixed expression of stubbornness. The edge of his jaws were sharp against the deeply tanned skin. The contradictions of character were evident; autocratic domination against his enemies and gentle patience for friends. His tenacity, faithfulness, and responsibility made him an individual

175

who men followed and looked up to. His great strength now was channeled toward hatred and the desire to get his hands on the evil which is so elusive. Ashton was tough, unyielding, and now dedicated to the destruction of Bullard and his outlaws. In good times and in bad, Ashton would never change much. His beliefs and feeling would remain the same. His pride would never let him step aside when trouble came.

Following the burial, Ashton, Rawlings, and Ben Mathews gathered in Ashton's study. He motioned the men to take comfortable chairs near the front window.

"Jeb, you once told us there is a way to get up behind the valley where Bullard and his men hide out."

"That's a fact," the old man said and nodded.

"Will you take us there?"

Rawlings had a bottle in one hand and a glass in the other. He was on his third bottle since arriving at the ranch the previous day but showed no real effect. He was drinking out of the glass merely out of courtesy, Ashton thought.

"Yup. Best not to take too many. We kin' be seen easy."

Ashton sat on the corner of his desk letting his left leg dangle.

"What about four of us, including you?"

Rawlings took a long drink and drained the glass.

"Yup."

Ashton rose and clasped his arms behind his back.

"This is what I have in mind. You men tell me what you think should be added to the plan and what should be changed," Ashton stated.

An hour and a half later the men emerged from the ranch house. Ashton issued orders to several men who saddled their horses and rode out. Ben Mathews took two men and headed for town with a wagon. A sense of purpose was in the air.

Ashton mounted his horse and struck out for town. He rode east through the gentle hills covered with the never-ending grass that carpeted the ground. The grass was broken only by a few lone trees standing as sentinels and an occasional pile of rocks. As he looked back at the ranch, the land rose step by step until it reached the foothills of the Owlhoots. In many ways it was a solitary land, and a lone rider accented the surrounding loneliness.

It was his land, and he now loved it with an intensity that few could understand. He was bound to it by the pain and struggle that had gone before and the hopes and dreams he had for the future. Its openness and freedom and its smells and colors were part of him now. These things comforted him, gave him a sense of fullfillment, and guided his destiny.

He reached the well-worn trail that entered town and fifteen minutes later rode slowly down the main street. He pulled up at Winters' store and dismounted. The last of the supplies he had ordered were being loaded into the ranch wagon by Mathews and his men.

"Any trouble?" Ashton asked.

"No. He filled the order without saying a

word."

Mathews slowly rolled himself a cigarette, and Ashton surmised he wanted to say more.

"Say what's on your mind, Ben."

He looked at Ashton and then back at the fixings.

"She's in there. I got the feeling she knows what the gunpowder is to be used for."

Ashton nodded his head as if to say he understood.

"Is she still going to leave?"

"I think so, Ben. That's what I'm here to find out."

The two men parted, and Ashton entered the store. She came to him and stopped just far enough away so that he could not touch her. The familiar fragrance of her hair revived his deep feelings. Her eyes held him and he could read the hurt and deep fear within them. She was silently pleading with him.

"A man has to do what he thinks is right," he said.

To her the words were a clear answer and a final refusal. Nothing would stop his course of action now. In looking at him and not speaking, she transmitted her bitter disappointment.

"I'm asking you not to go."

"I have to," she said.

Her simple response was enough. There was no other way open to him. The decision was made, there was no turning back, and the judgement was entirely his own. He lived by his code of self-reliance—iron-willed pride. Every person had to

178

make his own decision, and John Ashton had made his.

"I'll miss you," he said.

She just shook her head, and her long, brown hair framed her tanned face.

The following morning Charlie McGraw arrived at the Ashton Ranch with four of his riders. Ashton greeted the tall, bearded rancher and the two men went into the ranch house.

"Your man told me you want to take on Bullard" McGraw said. "He's a tough customer."

Ashton poured two cups of coffee and handed one to McGraw.

"All I ask is that you listen to my plan. If you like it, you are welcome to join us. If not, you and your men can ride home and there'll be no hard feelings," he explained.

Two hours later Race Jordan's men had arrived along with three from J. B. Michaels' ranch. Neither rancher would accompany the expedition, primarily because of age, he guessed. All afternoon the preparation continued. The men cleaned and loaded rifles, checked riding gear, loaded pack animals, and ate a big meal as dusk approached. Jeb Rawlings, for the most part, was content to sit on the front porch, swap stories, and drink.

15

Rawlings mounted his mule and departed as soon as darkness set in. The main body of riders left the ranch an hour later, and by nine were climbing the mountain trail single-file. There was no talking, and the riders cut a black outline against the pale night's sky. Small lights winked on the prairie below, showing the location of the main ranches in the area. It had been warm at the beginning of the trip, but as the procession wound slowly up into the mountains it became increasingly colder. Ben Mathews shivered and buttoned his heavy, sheep-lined coat. Other riders made similar gestures. At intervals Rawlings and his mule would suddenly materialize on the trail in front of the procession.

"So far, so good?" Ashton said quietly.

"Ain't a thing stirin'," the mountain man replied. "Keep 'em moving about this same speed. Rest when you have to. Any trouble, and you'll know it."

Rawlings abruptly pulled his mule about and quickly disappeared around a bend in the trail. The horsemen continued slowly upward, picking their way carefully in the dark. The clicking of metal horseshoes against rocks on the trail and the creaking of leather and harness were magnified in the still mountain air. Nineteen men and ten pack-horses comprised the group. The trail reached its peak and then started downward still winding through the pine trees and aspen. The fear of the unknown and the thought of being perfect targets in the night slowly began to leave the men as the ride became more routine. The trail entered a clearing with a small creek running through it, and the men dismounted and watered the horses. Those who smoked went in among the trees, rolled cigarettes, and carefully lighted them. They shielded the burning ends with their cupped hands, and from a distance only pale glows were visible. The acrid smell of burning tobacco spread over the clearing. Fifteen minutes later the men mounted and continued their journey. Downward they rode until they recrossed the same creek at the bottom of the canyon. The trail started upward again, this time on switchbacks that cut a zigzag course on the predominantly shale mountainside. The trail was not clear, and the men had to dismount and walk the horses. The men were tired, and the horses started to blow as they reached another summit point. Rawlings was waiting and talked quietly with Ashton as the men moved in among the trees to relax. It was after two in the morning, and the cold was seeping into the bones of the riders. They moved about stamping their feet and slapping themselves on the arms to keep warm.

Now Rawlings took the lead, and the party left the trail and picked its way through the forest along nearly unrecognizable animal trails. The going was difficult as animals and men continually brushed against the lower tree branches. When the foliage became extremely dense, the men were forced to dismount and lead the horses again. They walked on carpets of pine needles accumulated over dozen of years. Suddenly, looming out of the darkness, was a massive, grey shape. In front of the huge cliff face was an open area where the horses and mules were unsaddled and unloaded. By the time the men had finished eating, dawn was breaking. They had traveled all night over back trails and through thick pine forests to reach a sheltered, non-visible area located an hour's ride from the canyon opening leading to Bullard's hideout. They had arrived unseen and undetected.

The morning sunrise turned the clouds a bright orange along the horizon. Just before the sun became visible, the areas of open sky between the clouds turned a vivid pink-blue color. Ashton silently smoked as he viewed the panoramic scene. Rawlings approached him.

"It's 'bout time. Who's goin' with us?"

Ashton gestured toward the group of riders across the clearing.

"Randy Miller, the short rider over there who's the center of attention. He's good-natured and friendly and also tough."

Ashton called Miller over and introduced Rawlings to him.

"You men have been around each other from time to time but probably have never formally been introduced."

The two men nodded at each other and Miller smiled.

"I've watched you use that buffalo gun, Jeb. You do some fine shooting." Miller said.

"I just hang on to the back of it," Rawlings replied and grinned.

The three men mounted their horses and began to pick their way through the forest again. Rawlings led, followed by Ashton; Miller was last. Behind him was a pack mule loaded down with rope. The pines began to thin out as the men climbed higher. The going was slow because they stayed off even the trails that were not used often. Rawlings had explained that any droppings left by the animals on the trails might reveal their presence. About mid-day the three men had circled the necessary distance around behind Bullard's mountain hideout and now were prepared for the most difficult climb of all along bare ravines, up the shale mountain side and over rock slides.

The mountain formation was comprised of jagged pinnacles that jutted upward from the ground. The huge slabs of rock were separated by ravines that could have been knife cuts between the connected rock masses. The pointed rock formation looked as if it had been formed by a group of fingers pushing skyward out of the ground. This mountain section rose majestically hundreds of feet in the air.

Rawlings watched Ashton and Miller as they stood staring upward.

"Any questions?" the mountain man asked.

"Do we need wings?" Miller asked jokingly.

The pack mule was unloaded, and each of the men carried a heavy bundle of rope as they began the ascent up the first rock slide at the base of the cliffs. Their feet sunk deeply into the river of sand and small rocks, and headway was slow and painstaking. After arriving at the start of the first ravine, Rawlings pointed out the route to climb. Ashton began the climb with an ordinary lasso tied to his waist. He climbed the first thirty feet hand over hand, pulling himself upward foot by foot over the jagged rocks. When he reached an outcropping large enough to hold three people, he lowered the rope and pulled up the bundles of fiber cord, each an inch in diameter. Then Miller and Rawlings were hoisted up. The process was repeated several times until the men had reached the top of one of the jagged pinnacles.

"You kin' work your way along that narrow shelf until you git' there," Rawlings pointed out. "I tried two other ways that didn't work before I found this here route."

Ashton hugged the side of the cliff face as he inched forward. He was sweating heavily, partially from the exertion and partially out of fear. A drop of sweat rolled down his back between his shoulder blades, making him shiver. He could feel his hands sweating inside the gloves, and the perspiration was beginning to drop from his eyebrows on to his cheeks. The ledge finally ended in a gully and from there Ashton was able to climb higher in a half-circle until he was above his partners. He pulled the bundles of heavy rope up first and then the two men.

"Let me take the lead for awhile," Miller said.

Ashton reluctantly agreed, knowing he needed

184

relief. Miller successfully scaled the next one hundred feet in three intervals. The men took a lengthy rest in mid-afternoon and then continued their assault on the mountain. They finally reached a boulder-strewn incline that led them to the top. Nearly exhausted by the climb, they sat with their backs against a large rock and looked out over the countryside. The breathtaking view began with the trees below them, which flowed down the mountainside like streams of water twisting and turning over barren ground. They were higher than the surrounding mountain peaks, and the rocky crags appeared to gently flow away from them. Below the mountains the green and brown foothills gave way to a sea of yellow and reddish grass that stretched as far as the eye could see.

"I've never seen anything like it," Miller said quietly.

"An' some people wonder why I like to live in these here mountains," said Rawlings.

Ashton looked at him and smiled. "You don't have to convince me."

The men drank slowly from their canteens, rested a few minutes, and then climbed to a point where they could look down into the canyon which emptied into the huge meadow. Ashton studied the cluster of log buildings, the shape of the meadow, the corrals, the well, and the pasture land at the end of the meadow where the horses were kept.

"There are only three buildings that we need to worry about—the two bunkhouses and the main house," Ashton said.

He memorized the exact location of the buildings and instructed his companions to do the same.

"When we go in, it will be dark. We have to know exactly where to put the powder and where the men should take cover," Ashton explained.

They then turned their attention to the descent. It was impossible to hike around the top of the mountain formation because of the gaps and gorge-like breaches that slashed earthward for hundreds of feet before coming to abrupt endings. The heavy ropes would have to be utilized in climbing down into the meadow. Ashton studied the canyon walls until it was nearly dark and decided on a downward route. It was at the far end of the meadow behind the horse pasture.

Darkness settled in the canyon rapidly, and the three men pulled back from the edge of the rim to eat and watch the sun set. The sky filled with the red-orange glow of a southwestern sunset that gave all objects an eerie cast. Grey colors and then blackness mingled with the orange and fire-red colors. The mountains cut a black outline against the streaked sky. Ashton and Miller smoked their last cigarettes before the climb down began. Rawlings whistled softly to himself, rightfully unconcerned because he was not making the decent with the other two men. It had been decided that his buffalo gun could be used to best advantage at the top of the rim.

"You ready?" Ashton asked.

"Ready as I'll ever be. Maybe we can just slide down the rope all the way," Miller said jokingly as an afterthought.

"When you hit the bottom they'd probably hea

you all the way inside the cabin," Ashton replied and grinned.

Once the descent began all frivolity disappeared. The winds came up at dusk, causing the sweat-drenched men to shiver. Each man carried fifty feet of rope strapped to his body, and they used another length to lower themselves down the first thirty foot descent. This was followed by another descent of forty-five feet and another close to thirty feet. Each time the lasso was attached to a pointed outcropping. Ashton would snap the rope, and it would kick free of the rock after the two men had descended to another ravine, rock shelf, or edge. They carefully worked their way down the path Ashton had mapped out in his mind. Their only concern was the small pebbles and rocks that were kicked loose as they worked their way down. He counted on the fact that the meadow was more than a quarter mile in length, and the men in the canyon were not likely to be near the corrals after dark.

They reached a sheer rock face that stretched downward for more than one hundred feet. The three ropes were attached together, and Ashton slowly fed the line down the cliff face.

"Be careful," Miller said.

"Believe me, I will."

Ashton felt his arms tiring as he again lowered himself hand over hand, foot by foot, down the mountain. The cords in his arms ached, and the constant strain caused him to begin to shake. After twenty feet, he wrapped the rope around his foot several times and attempted to rest while clutching the rope. Then slowly he slid down the rope a foot or two at a time. The descent was easier, but the rope tended to twist and bang his knees or back into the mountain. Half way down, he again rested and wondered if he would make it. Sweat ran into his right eye, and the stinging sensation lasted for several minutes. He continued sliding down the rope and finally reached a shelf of layered rocks. Ashton looped the rope around his waist, pulled on the rope three times to signal Miller to begin his descent, and then lay down to rest. The moon was bright in a cloudless sky as he watched Miller come down the rope at a much greater speed. The thought passed through his mind that someone on the ground would be able to see them.

Miller reached the rock plateau and sat with his back against the mountain, too tired to move.

"God, but I'm tired," Miller admitted.

Ashton pulled himself to a sitting position. "I didn't think climbing this mountain and then lowering ourselves in would be so difficult."

"I don't care if I never see another mountain."

"Neither do I."

"Major, you have any water left? I'm about out."

"Here Randy. Don't call me Major. The war is over."

Miller drank deeply from the canteen that had been passed to him.

"How much longer will it take us?" Miller asked.

"I think we are about two-thirds of the way down. Another hour, anyway. We'll have to try and be as quiet as possible."

"Do people really climb mountains just for fun?" Miller asked.

The going became easier as the sheer drop-offs ended. Ashton sensed they could have climbed down the remaining two hundred feet, but lowering themselves with ropes was quieter. Ashton finally reached the ground only a short distance from the corrals. Miller joined him a minute later, and the two men coiled the ropes and hid them. They quietly circled the corrals in the opposite direction from the cluster of log buildings. In the moonlight, they could see various paths crossing the meadow. The two men stopped as they reached the mouth of the canyon that led to the outside.

"You think there'll only be one guard?" Miller whispered.

"No way of telling. We'll wait here behind these trees until the guard is changed and then decide what to do. Go to sleep for awhile. I'll stand watch."

Miller was asleep within minutes and Ashton struggled to stay awake. The stiffness had set in, and it was an effort to move any part of his body. The early morning coolness came, and the cold seeped into his bones. Ashton pulled the collar up on his jacket and crossed his arms. His clothing was still wet from perspiration and did little to hold the body heat. His mind cleared as he became colder.

Thirty minutes later he heard a man coming down the path that came from the north side of the canyon wall. The man walked rapidly down the rock trail, across the meadow and into the first bunkhouse. Five minutes later a different man emerged from the log building and shuffled slowly up the winding trail until he disappeared into the blackness at the top of the canyon wall.

If there is a second guard, Ashton thought, he will be coming within a few minutes.

The assumption was correct, as a man could be heard descending from the other side of the canyon. He, too, walked by Ashton's hiding place and entered the same building. Minutes later another man emerged from the bunkhouse. He had a deep racking cough and wheezed as he climbed the trail. Ashton pulled off his boots and quickly followed the outlaw. The path was fairly smooth, but occasionally Ashton would step on a sharp rock. The pain seemed to be intensified because of his weary condition, and it was all he could do to keep from crying out.

When the trail reached the top of the mountain formation, it proceeded to weave in and out among large boulders that were outlined against the pale night's sky. Ashton would run from the deep shadows of one boulder to the next as he followed the outlaw.

"That you, Starkey? a voice called from the other side of the canyon ridge.

"Yeah" said the man Ashton was following.

A spasm of coughing followed and lasted for more than a minute.

"What's wrong with you?"

"I don't know. The cold weather gets me cough ing."

The two outlaws were silent for a few minutes

"Why does Bullard want two of us to stan

guard?" Starkey asked.

"Can't say. He was up here this afternoon for a long time. They said he just kept studying the countryside. Nobody saw anything. He didn't see anything. Just jumpy I guess. Things ain't been going all that good."

"You're right," Starkey replied, and was racked with another coughing spell.

Their voices echoed in the canyon as they talked back and forth. Ashton silently made his way back down the trail to where Miller was still sleeping. He quietly woke his companion and explained what they would do.

"I can't ever remember feeling this bad," Miller whispered.

"I know."

"I'm freezing, my body hurts all over, and I'm so stiff I don't think I can get up."

"Other than that, how do you feel?" Ashton asked and grinned.

Miller groaned softly and struggled to bring himself to a standing position. He grabbed a tree limb for support. Fifteen minutes later the two partners started to climb the narrow trails on either side of the canyon passage that led to the outside. Now and then the jagged stones would penetrate his rocks making him want to cry out. He knew Miller was going through the same torture. When they reached the top, the two men moved silently from the deep shadows of one boulder to another.

As they neared the guards, they heard the outlaws talking across the gorge. Their voices echoed in the chasm. Ashton waited until the moon slid behind a cloud and then slowly crept to within twenty-five feet of the outlaw called Starkey.

Then what he was waiting for occurred. Starkey began coughing again, and Ashton quickly advanced to where the outlaw was sitting. Starkey was hacking, his arms resting on his knees and his face pointing towards the ground. Ashton brought the heavy revolver crashing down on his head, and the outlaw crumpled into a pile. With only a moment's pause, Ashton began coughing, trying to copy the outlaw's hacking sound. He lifted Starkey's surprisingly light body and carried it around behind some rocks. Since he could not distinguish the outlaw's clothing on the other side of the gorge, Ashton did not bother to put on Starkey's coat. He quickly walked along the path until he stood at the edge of the mountain cliff. Below him the low barrier of mountains cast black outlines in the pale night's sky.

Ashton began coughing again and in a choked voice called to the other outlaw.

"Hey! Is that a light down there?"

The other outlaw stood up and walked out to the cliff's edge.

"Where?" I don't see anything."

"Over there, straight out in front of you," Ashton replied.

The outlaw heard something at the last moment that made him swing around, but it was too late. Brandishing his rifle like a club, Miller swung a roundhouse blow that caught the guard along the left side of the face. The smack of metal against bone and flesh sent the outlaw's body shooting over the edge of the cliff. It bounced twice before hitting bottom.

Miller began swearing softly to himself.

"Are you alright, Randy?" Ashton asked.

"Yeah. I stubbed my toe on a big rock just before I hit him. Damn, my feet hurt."

Ashton reached into his pocket and pulled out a handful of matches. He lighted one, let it blaze for a moment, and then blew it out. He repeated the process four times. From the blackness below, answering lights were flashed.

Within fifteen minutes, the single file of men began walking up the narrow canyon carrying kegs of gunpowder, ammunition, water, and other supplies. They wound along the path for a quarter of a mile before coming to the end, where it emptied into the meadow. Ashton was waiting for them. He motioned for the cowboys to follow him, and they made their way into a small stand of trees just inside the meadow.

Mathews and Ashton conversed for several minutes. Then Mathews led a group of eight men towards one of the bunkhouses. They circled around the smaller bunkhouse and arrived at the northern most buildings, which housed the most men. Gunpowder was planted on all four sides of the rectangular building, with most of the barrels near the two doors. The men then stationed themselves behind a rock formation to the east of the building and behind a rise in the ground to the north.

Bill Autry led a second group of men on a similar mission to the smaller bunkhouse. Again the barrels of powder were placed on all four sides of the building. Two large concentrations were near each door. Several of the men stationed themselves in among some small trees to the west of the bunkhouse. Three other cowboys located themselves behind boulders to the south of the bunkhouse.

Ashton positioned five men around the main log house, which he was sure held Bullard and two or three men. Again the barrels of gunpowder had been placed strategically around the main house and were piled neatly on the front porch.

An hour before daylight, Mathews had circled around and joined Ashton to the south of the triangle of buildings, now completely circled with men.

"Are you making it, alright?" Mathews asked.

"I'll be fine. Need a little sleep, that's all."

Mathews stepped closer and in the bright moonlight could see the sweat shining on Ashton's face. He was about to speak, but Ashton cut him off.

"Do you see any weaknesses?"

Mathews hesitated a moment before he spoke. "The northeast corner heading off in the vicinity of the outhouse is the only open area. If they'd break from the bunkhouses, some of them might get to cover near the west wall. We can't cover everything. The powder should be the trick."

"I want to give them a chance to surrender. The idea of just blowing them up doesn't set right," Ashton told his foreman.

"To tell the truth, John, I don't really care. When they killed Jamie, I stopped thinking about fair play."

Ashton said nothing, and in the darkness Mathews could not discern his features. Mathews pulled the coat closer around his neck. The early morning dew coupled with a light fog gave the meadow a peaceful look.

But the pressures within the men were mounting. They knew the fighting would begin within the hour. Some would die. Each man knew it would not be him. It was a universal hope cherished by all civilized men just before battle. Yet in the early morning cold crept into the bones making men shiver.

John Ashton felt the numbness leaving him. As the sky became lighter, his senses became more alert. The buildings became more visible in the grey light. Ashton forgot about being tired and inspected his revolver and Winchester. Anytime now, he thought.

Minutes later a bearded man appeared in the doorway of the larger bunkhouse. He scratched himself, stretched, and walked towards the outhouse, wearing only his long underwear. After a short time, he walked back to the bunkhouse and stopped on the porch, when he noticed the barrels of gunpowder for the first time. Sleepy and confused, he looked at the barrels for several moments and then bent down to examine them more closely. Still not understanding what the gunpowder was doing next to the door, he stood up and put his hands on his hips. Suddenly, he stiffened as the first vestige of fear came over him. His head slowly turned and looked into the surrounding meadow. His eyes widened as fear gripped him. The bearded outlaw suddenly dove through the doorway, yelling as he hit the floor.

16

The larger bunkhouse came alive with men grabbing clothes and their weapons. Confusion reigned as men poked their heads out of the windows and door and withdrew when they saw the gunpowder. Two half-dressed men appeared in the doorway of the second bunkhouse. Ben Mathews, who had made a semi-circle and joined his men to the south of the bunkhouses, fired a shot that buried itself in the doorframe near the two men. They disappeared back inside.

"Who are you? What do you want?" a deep voice bellowed from the smaller bunkhouse.

"Alright, listen up in those buildings," Mathews yelled. "Throw out your guns and come out. We aim to take you back to town peaceably if we can. If not, we'll blow up the buildings. You got two minutes to think about it."

At the north end of the meadow, Ashton was lying behind a rock formation closest to the main house. The fog had cleared, and he could see plainly to the other end of the meadow where Mathews was protected behind a boulder. Ashton thought he detected movement within the log house but wasn't sure.

Suddenly a group of five men burst from the

doorway of the larger bunkhouse and ran towards the latrine. Seeing this, four men ran from the smaller bunkhouse toward a small stand of Aspen.

I knew they wouldn't surrender, Mathews thought, as he squeezed the trigger of his Winchester. The resulting explosion boomed across the meadow, sending a shower of wood raining down over the entire area. A cloud of smoke surged into the air, and the rolling mass billowed outward like a great wave.

A split second later, Ashton also fired, and the north end of the small bunkhouse disappeared in another cloud of smoke and fire. Bits and pieces of wood and other material rained down.

Both bunkhouses now were ablaze. Smoke from the explosions nearly hid the buildings from view. Inside the buildings the blasts had thrown the outlaws to the far ends of the buildings. Those standing near the point of the explosions merely disappeared. Wounded men were screaming and others attempted to crawl out the other sides of the bunkhouses.

The first group of men out the door of the larger bunkhouse were now undergoing a blistering fire as they ran to the shelter of the latrine. First one outlaw went down, wounded in the side, and then a second fell with a bullet in the hip. The second wounded outlaw emptied his revolver at the rise in the ground that hid the majority of Mathews' men. His diversion allowed the remaining three to reach cover behind the latrine. As he started to reload his gun, Mathews' bullet killed him.

But the outlaws had gained cover.

"Lord, but I don't see no way out for us," one outlaw lamented.

"Quit whinin'. If they catch us, it's the rope. We got nothing to lose," said an outlaw called Weasel Burke. His nose was a huge beak that angled down from a narrow face. "Let's get into them trees and then try to get around to the trail out of here."

Keeping the latrine between them and Mathews' concealed riders, the outlaws ran for the aspen.

At the same time, the four outlaws from the smaller bunkhouse also were running for the same trees which were defended by three cowboys. Ashton, who was sixty feet away, shot at the lead man and knew he hit him. The outlaw staggered but stayed on his feet. The tall aspen trees did not provide a great deal of protection for the cowboys, and as the outlaws converged on the trees a hail of bullets splattered around the defenders.

A cowboy named Gene Mosley fired at the lead outlaw in the second group, and this time the man went down. An instant later, Mosely took a bullet in the chest and dropped his rifle. He managed to pull his revolver out and fired at the first outlaw to reach the trees. The outlaw went down, but Mosely died seconds later as the other two outlaws entered the trees and shot the wounded cowboy.

Glen Edwards, another of the cowboys, had his attention directed to the other outlaws coming from the larger bunkhouse. So did his companion, Bill Fosse. As they blasted away with their rifles, two of the outlaws went down, but Weasel reached the trees and shot Fosse in the face as he dived for cover. A second slug fired by one of the other outlaws entered the back of Edwards' right shoulder.

Seeing what had transpired and that remnants of both outlaw groups had reached the trees, Ashton and Randy Miller ran toward the trees. Ben Mathews and two of his men also were running in the direction of the aspen. The three outlaws retreated deeper into the trees, firing as they ran. It now became a deadly fight among the trees. A target would momentarily become visible and then be blocked out. The low tree branches got in the way of a man swinging his rifle from target to target. As the cowboys got closer to the outlaws, they drew their revolvers for the final confrontation.

One of the outlaws went to his knees as a slug smashed into his right shoulder. He took a second bullet and rolled over. A second outlaw was firing his revolver as fast as he could in the direction of Ashton and Miller as Ben Mathews stepped out from behind a tree. He took careful aim and fired. The outlaw was knocked off his feet by the force of the bullet entering his head.

Weasel Burke was down behind a log. He snapped a shot at one of his pursuers, and the shot splattered splinters of wood from the tree in the face of the cowboy. His second shot struck another cowboy in the shoulder. In a flash, he was on his feet and darting back among the trees until he reached the canyon wall and then circled to the canyon passageway that led to the outside.

A cowboy, stationed up on the trail that led

along the canyon wall which guarded the passage out, drew a bead on Weasel.

"Stop!" he yelled.

But Weasel's mind was fixed on only one thing—escape. His headlong flight could not be deterred, and he ran down the passage like a wounded animal trying to escape a pack of dogs. The cowboy on the rim braced his rifle against a boulder, held his breath, and fired. The Winchester bucked, and Weasel landed in a spread-eagled position, his lifeless eyes looking down the trail.

Jess Bullard had been moving from window to window in the log house looking for an opportunity to break for freedom. He viewed the explosions with surprise that bordered disbelief. His base of power had just been blown to pieces before his eyes. But the animal instinct for survival quickly took over. He watched the two groups of outlaws rush from the bunkhouses and sensed that his chance was at hand. He saw Ashton and Miller break from cover and head for the trees. Bullard turned and lunged out the back door, moving at surprising speed for his size. He grunted as he ran toward the east canyon wall.

Two cowboys were concealed behind the rock formation that Bullard was charging. Both men were looking at the action in the trees across the meadow, and Bullard was practically on top of them before they reacted. The outlaw leader carried a revolver in each hand and emptied one gun at the cowboys as he reached the rocks that stood in front of the canyon wall. His six shots ricocheted off the rocks, and a rock fragment struck one of the cowboys in the right eye. The other cowhand fired his revolver twice, and his second shot struck Bullard as the outlaw leader gained cover behind the rocks. Bullard's single-minded determination kept him rushing onward around the rock formation, the boulders, and into a ravine cut into the canyon wall. The ravine twisted and turned as it went higher up the canyon wall, and in a moment Bullard was out of sight and climbing.

Ashton emerged from the trees on the far side of the meadow in time to see Bullard gain the safety of the rocks. He raced over to the two cowboys. One was wrapping the other cowhand's eyes with a bandage.

The cowboy looked up guiltily.

"We just didn't see him until he was on top of us. I hit him. I know I did. It didn't seem to even slow him down."

"I'll take care of him," Ashton said. In a crouching position he ran to the ravine entrance.

As quickly as the battle began, it ended. Twelve dazed and wounded outlaws had struggled from the burning bunkhouses before they were totally consumed in flames. The exploding timber had peppered the outlaws with projectiles and splinters. Those men not seriously injured physically, were dazed from the shock of the explosion. Several were lying on the ground, covering their ears with their hands. Others were covered with powder and smoke marks. The large ring of cowboys slowly advanced into the center of the meadow.

They searched the remaining buildings and log house, but no more adversaries were found. Attention then was turned to administering first aid to the wounded cowboys, and then the outlaws.

Ben Mathews' full attention was directed towards organizing the cowboys' movements, and it was not for several minutes that he realized John Ashton was missing.

"Hold it!" he yelled. "Who has seen John Ashton?"

The cowhand who had wounded Bullard stepped forward.

"He followed Bullard up into the rocks. I shot him, but he still got by us."

Mathews stared at the man, an incredulous look on his face, then quickly motioned to three cowboys standing in a group.

"Bullard's in the rocks somewhere. Find him. This man will show you where to start," Mathews ordered.

The cowboys ran toward the canyon wall.

Jess Bullard, like a lumbering giant, pulled and clawed his way upward along the ravine in the canyon wall. The passageway became wider and was filled with rocks and boulders of all sizes and dimensions, deposited by rushing water during the rainy season. The huge man was bleeding heavily from the wound in his side, but it did not seem to hinder or slow him down. He clawed at the rocks for hand holds as he struggled higher. Reddish-brown dust began to coat his face, beard, and dark clothing. He finally reached a level area and stopped momentarily to rest. His wheezing was the only noise among the rocks.

After a few moments, he was in motion again. Years before he had followed this escape route until it reached the top of the canyon wall. From there it would be relatively easy to hide in the mountains until pursuit ended. The ravine was out of sight of those in the canyon interior and was known only to Bullard. The path led over rock formations, around outcroppings, and through rock slides. He began to tire, and his progress was slower. Bullard reached another flat area and slumped to the ground, his back against a large rock. Sweat dripped from his massive eyebrows onto his cheek and made small rivers through the caked dust. His hard breathing made a whistling noise, and his mouth hung open. Bullard's animal-like eyes darted along the ravine below him, searching. After a few minutes he relaxed and his eyes began to close. He had to fight with himself to stay awake. Pulling out a revolver, he reloaded the weapon and then repeated the procedure with his second gun.

Glancing back down the ravine, Bullard suddenly became fully awake. Before he could see the man, he saw the dust rising as Ashton scrambled up a narrow rock slide.

It's Ashton, Bullard thought. I know it's him. He experienced a feeling of elation. The thought of killing Ashton before he escaped was overpowering to the outlaw leader. Keep coming, he thought. Keep coming.

A figure took shape out of the dust. Ashton

moved cautiously from boulder to boulder. His eyes continually scanned the rocks above him as he climbed. Ashton suddenly knew Bullard was watching and waiting. He instinctively felt the other man's eyes on him. He wiped the sweat from his eyes, caught his breath, and continued. There is no alternative, he thought.

The distance between the two men narrowed. Bullard became anxious. His eyes gleamed. His fingers tightened on the revolver. The big man was totally consumed with the idea of killing his foe. A rumbling sound came from deep within his chest as Ashton reached another open rock slide area. Ashton paused, and then started upward, his boots sinking into the sand and rocks. For every two feet he went forward, he slid back one foot.

Bullard fired, and the explosion ricocheted off the rock walls. The bullet whistled past Ashton's right ear, and he dove to one side. Seeing the powder, he fired twice with his repeating rifle. The shots smashed into the boulder shielding the outlaw leader, and Bullard was on his feet again. He ran around a bend in the ravine and was instantly out of sight. Ashton laboriously climbed the forty five yards to Bullard's hiding place. In the distance he could hear Bullard kicking rocks loose as he climbed. Ashton noticed that the trail of blood spots was becoming harder to follow, indicating that the bleeding probably would stop. He glanced around the edge of a rock formation, could see nothing above him, and started to climb again.

The two men kept their relative positions and climbed steadily upward for the next half hour

The ravine finally gave way to a wide, boulder-strewn mountain side near the peak. Bullard wanted to pick his location for a surprise shot and was hidden by the time Ashton came into view. The bleeding had stopped, and he had had a chance to catch his breath before Ashton reached the boulder field. Now Ashton sat down and rested.

The ranch owner surmised that the running was over. Bullard would make his last stand here. The odds were in Bullard's favor. The outlaw was waiting in ambush, and Ashton would have to probe and search for him.

John Ashton took a deep breath, crouched down, and began to move in a semi-circle through the maze of huge boulders and rock formations scattered along the top of the canyon wall. Sweat poured down his face and upper torso. Every sense was alert as his eyes moved from rock to rock. He heard Bullard coming from behind a huge rock formation directly behind Ashton.

Ashton froze momentarily, and then threw himself sideways as Bullard fired. He rolled behind a rock projection and was quickly on his feet. Bullard had again missed and quickly disappeared. Ashton circled the outlaw's last location and came up behind a large flat boulder. He put his foot into a crack, pushed himself upward, and grabbed a hand hold. Ashton then pulled himself up to a small ledge and from there climbed to the top of the flat rock. He stayed on his haunches, rifle in a ready position, and surveyed the field of rocks below him. Ashton put the rifle to his shoulder, rose to a

205

standing position, and spotted Bullard as the out-law ran along the rim of the canyon wall.

Ashton fired, and the outlaw leader stopped running. His mouth fell open and his eyes wide-ned. Ashton instantly levered another such round into the chamber and fired a second time as Bullard stumbled and fell over the ledge. His body hurtled through the air down into the canyon toward the remnants of his hideout.

The cowboys worked through the afternoon raz-ing the buildings, burying the dead outlaws, and destroying everything they could not take with them. Five of the healthiest outlaws were sent under guard to Desert City. Summerville's small jail could not accomodate them all. Two of the cowhands were dead—their bodies were sent back to their ranches. Three wounded cowboys were transported to town for medical attention from Doc Henderson. The remaining body of men, together with seven outlaws, left the canyon shortly before nightfall and camped in a lower mountain meadow. Two of the severely wounded outlaws died during the night, and a third the following morning.

Jeb Rawlings and John Ashton stood drinking coffee as they looked out over the surrounding mountains and grasslands in the far distance. The higher levels of mountains had a blue cast while the lower levels blended the greens of the trees and plants with various brown and red rocks.

"Will you ride back with us?" Ashton asked.

Rawlings poured another healthy measure of

whiskey into the tin coffee cup and then returned his gaze to the panoramic view.

"That there's your answer. Why would anybody want to live in this town?" Rawlings said, grinning.

"I see your point."

Rawlings' eyes twinkled.

"But I'll be paying you visits now and then, especially when you serve such good liquid."

The two men laughed.

Rawlings and his mule left the long line of men when they reached the foothills. As they traveled across the grasslands towards town, Ashton began to think of Ann Winter. His sense of well-being began to leave him as he thought of the woman he loved and knew was lost to him. Her long, golden-brown hair framing the deeply tanned oval face came sharply into focus. A feeling of emptiness came over him, and his stomach turned sour as he neared town. Was it all worth it? he thought. Was she right?

People lined both sides of the main street as the procession entered town. Ashton experienced the distasteful feeling of being part of a gruesome display or sideshow, and the expression on his face hardened.

"Move aside there!" he growled, when one segment of the crowd came too close to the line of horsemen.

Ashton glanced at the general store, and a look of shock passed over his face. Ann Winter stood in the doorway.

He turned in the saddle and looked at Ben

Mathews, who by this time was smiling.

"Take over, Ben," he said. He guided his horse to an open spot at the hitching rail.

Ann Winter disappeared inside the store, and Ashton quickly followed. His heart was pounding as he caught up with her.

"You didn't go!" he yelled.

She looked deeply into his eyes, and it was as if he could read her thoughts.

"I realized I couldn't. I love you, John. I had to wait to find out if you were alright."

He crossed the distance between them, took her in his arms, and kissed her long and hard. She responded totally, and for the two of them time stopped.

"You'll never have to wait again, Ann."